MURDER OF A PROPHET

The Dark Side of Utah Polygamy

A Fact-Based Novel

John R. Llewellyn

Agreka Books

Salt Lake City, Utah

Murder of a Prophet: The Dark Side of Utah Polygamy
by John R. Llewellyn

International Standard Book Number: 188810693X
Library of Congress Catalog Card Number: 99-068880

The author has portrayed his view of the current condition of Utah
polygamy in this fictional novel. The opinions expressed by the
characters in this book come from the author's experience and may or
may not reflect the actual opinions of Independent Fundamentalists,
Organized Fundamentalist groups, or The Church of Jesus Christ of
Latter-day Saints. Any similarity between the fictional characters and
actual people is coincidental.

For additional information see: www.utahbooks.com

800 360-5284
www.agreka.com

Acknowledgements

A special thanks to Linda Taylor, editor of Agreka Books, for her hard work, inspirational confidence, professional courtesy, publishing know how, and just being a beautiful lady. Every writer should be so lucky.

For those who seek more information about the history of polygamy in Utah, the following Internet Sites are suggested:
http://users.deseretonline.com/brianh/
http://www.mormonpolygamistcults.net

Chapter One

MARVIN SURVEYED his kneeling family, their heads and shoulders bowed, not saying a word, waiting to see who first would be permitted to rise. The only sounds came from the whimpering of Carolyn's three-month-old baby girl. With her head still bowed, Carolyn unbuttoned her dress, pulled aside the bra and began nursing the baby.

Marvin Heywood said, "Amen," and slowly rose to his feet while his five wives and thirty-one children remained kneeling, all facing the direction of the sacred Salt Lake Temple. In the Heywood home, morning family prayer was a daily ritual and at the end of each kneeling prayer, no one was permitted to stand without first getting Marvin's permission.

It was the Sabbath and the wives and children were clothed in their Sunday best, which meant their faces were clean and the ankle-length, cotton dresses of the girls and long-sleeved shirts of the boys had been washed but not necessarily ironed. Marvin's family survived only a notch above the necessities of life. When they could, the wives worked at odd jobs, mostly housework, otherwise their time was taken up giving birth to children, changing diapers, repairing the family station wagon, and working at keeping their own home. Marvin Heywood was the exception among polygamists rather than the rule.

The bulk of the Heywood food came from garbage Dumpsters behind grocery stores. Three times a week two wives with three or four of the older children gathered behind the local grocery stores and collected discarded vegetables, out-of-date bread, and damaged can goods. But with advanced technology, large supermarket chains enclosed

John R. Llewellyn

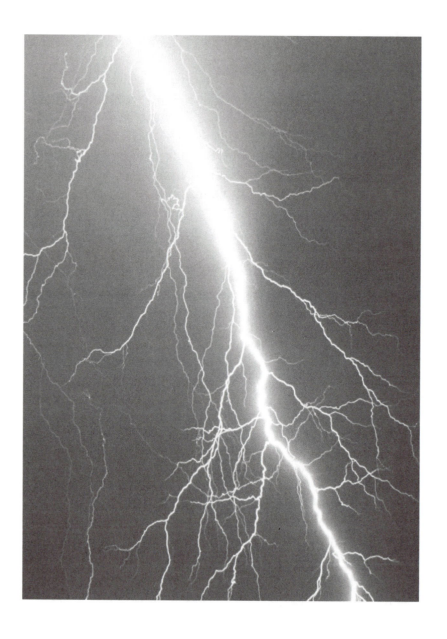

their Dumpsters, which put the Heywood women out of business.

Out of desperation, Ramona, the eldest wife, approached the produce manager of a new supermarket and asked if he would save his old produce for her goats and pigs. He was a large man with a bulbous nose and stern face. At first he hesitated, but after scrutinizing Ramona's paltry appearance, surrounded by three poorly-dressed but well-behaved kids, he agreed to place lettuce, apples, bananas, or whatever, in boxes so she could pick them up on Tuesdays and Fridays of each week.

During her bedtime prayers, Ramona asked God to bless the produce manager. Eventually, she discovered his name was Mac and routinely instructed her children at bedtime, "Don't forget to ask God to bless Mac."

Last Christmas, she and the children made Mac a large Christmas card out of colored paper and bits of ribbon. The children drew pictures of Christmas trees, snowmen, and goats. They all chipped in with their nickels, dimes, and quarters to buy a $6.99 brown and yellow tie for Mac and they wrapped it in glossy green paper with a red ribbon. When eight-year-old Judy handed Mac the package, he said it was the finest present he had ever received. Judy beamed with delight.

Then suddenly Mac was transferred to another store far away, too far for Ramona to drive. His replacement told Ramona he didn't have time to save vegetables for goats, and he wasn't in the welfare business.

The family had grown dependent upon Mac. More often than not on Tuesdays and Fridays when Ramona and the kids had picked up the precious boxes, they found apples and oranges in perfect condition, every bit as good as the ones on the shelves. Mac acted disinterested and aloof, but she knew he cared and she didn't think for a minute he believed they raised goats because every once in a while, hidden in the bottom of the boxes, they found bags of candy.

It had taken much courage to approach Mac. Now Ramona didn't know if she could do it a second time. Mac's replacement sneered at her in disgust. The guilt she felt from his cold stare was more than she could take. Marvin encouraged her to solicit other grocery stores and guaranteed that God would prepare the way by softening the hearts of the produce managers. This was Marvin's way of placing upon Ramona the burden of providing food for the family. If she could not find another Mac, they would have to make do with charity from the other group members and the meager stipend Marvin received from the priesthood. Reprimanding Ramona, he said, "Public welfare is out of the question," his chief fear being found out a polygamist by the government. What he didn't know is that because of their conspicuousness, the government already knew how they lived and was watching and waiting to see if Marvin's wives and children were being neglected or abused. The Division of Child and Family Services remained poised, eager to pounce once a complaint, no matter how trivial, could be substantiated.

Marvin had taught them obedience. They had been taught it was he, by virtue of his priesthood authority, who would supervise their resurrection on judgement day. Without him, they had no celestial exaltation, no opportunity to live with God one day. Therefore, after each kneeling family prayer, in a habit uniquely adopted by Marvin, he methodically determined who should rise first. It was no mere trivial ritual, but a symbolic exercise of judgement and resurrection. Consequently, Marvin carefully weighed the conduct, obedience, and usefulness of each family member before allowing him or her to rise and be "resurrected" each day.

As he surveyed the backs and elbows of his family, Marvin finger-brushed his bristly, light brown mustache. It was the same color as the little hair remaining around his ears and on the back of his neck. Standing before the mirror he routinely preened and trimmed for an hour three times a week, thinking that he and his mustache were comparable to Errol Flynn, his favorite movie actor. But Marvin in no way physically resembled Errol Flynn, not even with the help of his beloved mustache; it was out of character with his pink, square balding head that matched his fleshy, rectangular torso. He routinely wore brown baggy pants and a loose fitting, unstarched white dress shirt that never looked quite clean. This morning he sported a brown and yellow-striped necktie smudged with dried food stains.

To others, Marvin looked unkept, but because of his brilliant and articulate knowledge of the scriptures, his shabbiness was passed off as eccentricity. Marvin's research of old church doctrines and their application to modern times was unparalleled by any other member of the group. In fact, he was mentor to the serious students of the mysteries of Mormonism and they gathered around him like groupies to attend his study sessions and fireside chats. Marvin, a "man of words," was a self-made scholar who could always ferret out doctrine to justify any prudent contingency. But when it came to physical labor, he made a dramatic ceremony with gasps, groans, and feigned backaches.

Marvin could see that kneeling Carolyn was uncomfortable nursing her baby. It tempted him to allow her to rise first, but he did not, because he was afraid it would send to the others the wrong message. He was not ready to forgive her of her impertinence and disobedience. The swelling about her eyes had disappeared, but a black and blue mark could still be detected on her cheek bone. A fortnight ago, she had gotten hysterical and slandered him unmercifully until he smacked the side of her head with the butt of his hand. To hit anyone, let alone a woman, insulted his breeding, since Marvin considered himself a humble man of God. It angered him more that she had provoked him into violence than did her scolding, unprecedented verbal attack. But her haranguing was more than he could endure. Suddenly, with clenched fists, he flailed with all his might until she lay bleeding and unconscious at his feet. As he towered over her, glaring down with contempt, he almost shouted, "you filthy bitch," but he would not allow himself to stoop to profanity. He told himself she had it coming. After all, he could not stand there idly and allow her to call him a "no-good father who refused to work and feed his children." He had tried to explain in his most ingratiating, academic demeanor that if she had sufficient faith, her children would not be hungry, but she kept shouting and tearing at her clothes like a maniac. It was for her own good that he smote her.

And this is what he told Brother Harold, his priesthood head and prophet, who at first was upset, but later agreed. "Keep her inside until the bruises disappear," he reluctantly advised.

Marvin gazed down at Cynthia, his youngest wife. He had married her when she was sixteen. Since their marriage, she had mothered four lovely children and at age twenty-five still retained her girlish figure, while his other wives had accumulated ugly pounds. Even now, Cynthia, three months pregnant, didn't show. He thought of her as his geisha wife, one who had been raised, trained, and prepared to be an affectionate, obedient plural wife. Cynthia gave him much pleasure.

Marvin desired at least two more wives. After Cynthia, he concluded that young wives, at the age of puberty or soon thereafter, made the best wives. Between fourteen- and sixteen-years old they were suggestible and malleable and had not yet formed false opinions or sexual inhibitions. At that tender age, he formulated in his deluded mind, he could indoctrinate them with the servilities of womanhood and the idiosyncrasies of service to husband and priesthood. He could teach them that copulation is what bonds a woman to her husband. And he recalled, when teaching these things to

Cynthia, how virile and potent he felt in her presence, and the feeling of omnipotence that engulfed him. It was as if he were a God, her God, with the power to give life or take life.

Marvin did not know of the medical books describing pedophilic behavior and that his thoughts and acts were in classic conformance with those perverse aberrations. Nor did he realize that his demented mind produced lewd thoughts and images of children to cover up his great agony of sexual inadequacy experienced around mature, adult women. Naive combatants of child molestation reasoned that prostitution would alleviate and defuse the pedophile. But how could a super sex symbol like a prostitute erase that inability to perform? Marvin sensed that adolescent girls could not detect those feelings of inadequacy and therefore he performed without fear of exposure. He knew that what he was doing was wrong, but because his confidence was uplifted and exhilarated while in the pedophilic mode, he rationalized around his sickness and suppressed his guilt.

Religion and plural marriage provided the means in which to accomplish his erotic departure from the norms. It was not planned, it just worked out that way. Like thousands before him and thousands that would follow, he found opportunity in religion that could be twisted to conform with his distorted desires. So intense were his aberrations that he believed his own delusions, thinking his acts were sanctioned by God. But where Marvin lusted for little girls, others lusted for power and money, and they used religion like a loaded gun to coerce and manipulate the world around them.

Overwhelmed by satisfaction induced by Cynthia and thinking he could triple his erotic pleasure, Marvin approached the fathers of two sweet lasses and informed them that the Lord had made it known to him that their dainty and charming daughters should be his wives, surmising that his exalted apostleship would be flattering enough to induce the fathers to agree. He was deeply disappointed when his virtuous overtures were rejected by the two spirited young ladies. He couldn't understand why they didn't leap at the chance to share in his elite station or why their fathers did not exhort and cajole their compliance. But the fathers left the decision to the girls who said that *if and when* the Lord revealed to them that they belonged to Marvin Heywood, *and only then, maybe they would consider it.*

Piqued and perturbed by their impertinence, he suggested that Harold might command the fathers and the girls in the name of the Lord to acquiesce to his revelation. But Harold defended the free agency of the girls and that ended the matter.

Marvin blamed the insolence of the two young girls and the younger generation in general on the liberal climate that had been percolating in the group since Harold had opened the doors to new converts fifteen years ago. At that time, the McCallister group had approached Harold offering to merge, suggesting that Harold be the spiritual leader while Bruce McCallister handled the economic pursuits. But Harold rejected that offer. The McCallisters were suspected of inbreeding with cousins and half-sisters and Harold wanted no part of it.

The McCallister group, a closed ultra-private society, had reached the point where they had no other place to go for wives, but inside their own families. They told themselves that their McCallister blood was noble and pure, so it would be alright to marry within the fifth consanguinity. And so the anomaly was permitted, but only among the hierarchy. The McCallister boys took for wives their nieces, cousins, and half-sisters. Harold rightly predicted that one day they would be scandalized and branded with the indelible iron of incest. And he predicted that soon they too, as a group, would be faced with the same damning perplexities, unless they opened their doors to new converts and welcomed fresh blood.

So far, the Barnett sect had married each other's daughters and sisters until there was none left without crossing over that taboo line. So when Harold threw open the doors, the new converts brought with them liberal ideas like fashionable clothes, sporty cars, airplanes, and luxury homes. The more affluent frequented nice restaurants, attended movies and theater. A shyster type convert penetrated the Barnett ranks, a breed of businessmen proficient in the scriptures as well as the ways of the world. They were rainbow chasers teeming with schemes and conspiracies designed to separate honest men from their wealth.

In a matter of a few years, except for the fundamentalist-born who held fast to the old ascetic ways, one could not tell a Barnett polygamist from a gentile or orthodox Mormon. What a shame, Marvin thought, if fundamentalism were still managed like in the past, there would be no insubordination and those two pretty lasses he coveted would be his wives, and very pregnant.

The Grass Valley group in southwestern Utah, he mused, had not deviated from the old ways. Their women still favored the fashions of the twenties and thirties, and wore with pride the homespun, outdated ankle-length dresses. Their long hair, neat and clean with frilly bows and conservative combs, imitated the coiffures of the twenties.

The Grass Valley women in many ways resembled the modest, Pennsylvania Amish. Marvin found their bland appearance paradoxically appealing because their outward semblance was devoid of sexual intimidation, therefore unthreatening to his masculinity. The homely attire also bore collateral advantages. It discouraged erotic interest from outsiders, detoured waywardness, and tended to unite the women behind the priesthood. Besides, he satirically thought, when you get a woman all soaped up in a bathtub, you can't tell by looking if she was rich or poor, sophisticated or naive, polygamist or monogamist.

According to Marvin Heywood, the Barnett Group should be more like the Grass Valley people. At Grass Valley, when a maiden matured and was capable of giving birth, she presented herself to the priesthood and was placed by divine inspiration into the family where she belonged. A difference in age between the husband and the wife was of no consequence. Therefore a sixteen-year-old girl married to a fifty-year-old man was not uncommon. In some sects, when a wife was no longer of child bearing age, if the husband could influence the prophet, he took a new younger wife. It was the raising up of a righteous seed that was important, not lust. In essence, the infallible priesthood arranged for all women to unite with righteous men and raise up, in the name of Jesus Christ, a superior race of offspring. The parents' reward would come in the next life where they would rule as kings and queens, priests and priestesses over a subservient, white-skinned nation.

Marvin's melancholy mind went back to the women and children kneeling on the floor. "Cynthia," he said, "you may rise—and your children with you."

Carolyn and Rachel were among the last left kneeling. Carolyn, because she was still being punished, and Rachel, the third oldest daughter of Luwana his second wife, because he liked the shape of her buttocks. Rachel, who had physically matured early, would soon be sixteen. Marvin paid particular attention to her development. Of all his daughters, she was the most liberal, easily influenced, and his favorite. For some reason he didn't mind her open-mindedness, a puzzling reaction on his part considering that in every other respect he was a staunch conservative. Nor did he require her to dress as modestly as the other girls.

After everyone was finally standing and the mothers separated to go about their pre-church chores, Marvin approached Rachel who was changing a stinky diaper on a sibling, and said in his fatherly voice, "Rachel, there is something I need to talk to you about, would you please come with me?"

Rachel closed the bedroom door behind her and stood patiently while her father sat on the bed facing her. She knew the routine. Her long auburn hair, held together with a silver comb, had been piled high on her head, exposing the delicacy of her ears and neck. Her flawless tanned skin allowed dark full eyebrows and pink lips to dominate her pretty face. The nose, turned up pixie-like, give her profile a Scottish richness.

"How did it go last night?" he asked. "Did you do as I instructed?"

"Yes, Father," she replied.

"Did he touch you on the breasts?"

"Yes."

"Did he try to put his hands inside your blouse?" She was not offended by his questions; they had discussed beforehand what might happen. This was her third home date with Kevin Crutchfield.

"Yes, but I made him stop just like you told me," she said with a smile.

"Good girl, maybe next time we'll let him touch some skin. How did he act?"

"He started breathing real hard, was real nervous, and I think he almost asked me to marry him." She smiled, pleased with her accomplishments.

"Good, good," Marvin responded excitedly. "It sounds as if it won't be much longer before he asks me for your hand in marriage. That's when I tell him about the dowry."

Rachel nervously shuffled her feet. "Father, the dictionary says it's the woman who gives the man a dowry."

"Not in this case, honey," Marvin answered with a grin as he jauntily brushed his Errol Flynn mustache. "If Kevin wants my daughter for a plural wife, he's going to pay a dowry. After a couple more dates he'll want you so bad, he'll think $3000 is a bargain."

"But, Father, I don't want to marry Kevin, his breath stinks."

"You won't have to marry him, honey, I know of someone else interested in you who has more money than Kevin. Rachel," Marvin commanded, "take off your blouse and bra so I can see how you are developing."

"No, please."

Her opposition always startled him. After all, he was her God and she should not question any of his commands. But Rachel was the exception, the one he allowed to think for herself. She was the adventurous one, who didn't hesitate to accept a dare and seemed to mature socially at the same pace as her body. But she was sickened by his advances and recoiled as he reached with his hand.

And then he pulled a magazine from under the pillow that had been turned to a photograph of a naked women. He handed the magazine to Rachel, "This is what we hope you will look like when you're eighteen."

She glanced at the photograph of a young, dreamy-faced brunette lying naked on a bed. After a quick embarrassing look, she handed the magazine back and did her best to feign indifference. Finally, after what seemed like hours but was less than three minutes, he told her she could go back downstairs. As she started to leave, he said, "Tell Cynthia to come here, I want to talk to her.

A few minutes later Cynthia stepped into the bedroom. "Lock the door," he ordered while peeling off his shirt.

After each noxious episode with her father, Rachel suffered mood changes shifting from abject guilt to a sense of omnipotence over men. When she entered the family room, depression overcame her. Two adolescent girls sat against one wall thumbing through a stack of coloring books. One of the girls held Carolyn's crying baby, rocking back and forth.

Tears ran down his cheeks, mixing with snot from his nose. Three boys played with toy cars in a corner. One of the boys ran his car through a frayed tear in the carpet, pretending it was a gully. The flowered, threadbare carpet hadn't been cleaned for weeks and reeked of urine.

Two tattered overstuffed sofas and two dilapidated chairs, gifts from friends, were as frazzled as the carpet. Tina, Marvin's fourth wife, sat in one of the sofas, wrestling with a screaming, squirming little boy as she attempted to change his diaper. The rest of the furniture consisted of two rickety wooden chairs, one lay on its side and a kneeling boy used the other as a desk for his coloring book.

This is how each day goes—Rachel thought to herself—unchanging from dawn to dark, rags, dirty diapers, and urine stench. And this is my future if I stay.

She had to agree that Brother Harold was a kind, likeable man, but wondered if he had any idea that her father was teaching her how to tantalize and seduce rich men until they ached with a compulsion to bed her, and how he traded her affections for a dowry. She didn't think he knew or would approve, and many times after Marvin had pulled her blouse to one side so he could look down at her chest, she had been tempted to tell Brother Harold. She was certain that Brother Harold would end her father's debauchery, but if she informed on him, it might taint her chances to leave the group. The police and Division of Family Services might be notified, making matters worst, thwarting her chances to escape. She decided she could handle her father.

Convinced that her body was the ticket out of the group, she promised herself she would defect as soon as she found the right man. When she was ready, she would not run to the LDS Church like so many other fundamentalist traitors. She longed for excitement and adventure. In the meantime, if things got worse, she could always earn money posing like the women in her father's nudity magazines. And then in a temperament of self-deprecation, she pictured herself even further down the road of degradation. "I'll show him. I'll become a prostitute and make great sums of money." And as this thought lingered, she raised her fantasized future up a notch, and vowed not to become a common street harlot, but a fancy, expensive women of the night.

Disgusted with the dirty dishes piled high in the sink, the perpetual trash heap on the kitchen floor, the moldy food in the fridge and the mice smells, Rachel walked out to the front porch hungering for fresh air.

The September sun warmed the morning air. She pulled the comb from the auburn swirl and shook her head, glossy hair cascading down around her shoulders. She stood on the wooden platform that served as a porch and admired the neighbor's beautiful manicured yard next door; their garden overflowed with squash, cabbage, and tomatoes in the back yard. During the summer, the Samaritan neighbor unselfishly shared his garden bounty with the Heywoods.

Someday—Rachel told herself—I will have a nice home and garden and will spend my mornings talking with the little birds, smelling the bright gold and red flowers, munching on juicy red tomatoes.

Her reverie was shattered by one of her younger brothers running and laughing and jumping over a pile of rotting lumber in the front yard. Another brother ran in pursuit, shaking a stick in his hand as tears gushed from his eyes. She looked around at her own front yard. There was no grass or flowers, only hard-packed dirt and thirsty weeds fed by rainwater. Trash and debris lay everywhere. Two old cars with flat tires rusted away where a flower patch once grew. The neighbors on both sides had built sturdy, six-foot fences, not to block her view, but to block their view of the Heywood mess. The exhilaration of fresh air and flowers left her. Taking a lock of auburn hair, she wiped away the tiny rivulets running down her cheeks and stepped back into the house.

Chapter Two

MARVIN ACCESSED THE two-story red brick house by the back door, passed through the kitchen and entered the conference room by a side door. Harold Barnett sat at the head of the large, polished oak table. His younger brother, Calvin, seated at his right, glanced up from the papers in his hands. "Marvin, glad you made it, we were about to begin without you."

The family resemblance between Harold and Calvin was unmistakable in spite of having different mothers. Rotund in build, both were blessed with sparkling sky blue eyes and eternal optimism. Their jolly Santa Claus mien disarmed even the most severe critics. Harold, the older by three years, presided as the anointed leader over this polygamist group, The Apostles of Jesus Christ, affectionately referred to by members as the AJC.

Only a few members of the group knew the formal name of AJC or that it had been filed with the State of Utah as a non-profit religious corporation with tax exempt status. It wasn't that Harold necessarily wanted to keep the full name from the membership; the decision to keep quiet about it evolved from a need-to-know basis and to placate Richard Partridge. With corporate power, the priesthood could dispose of the hundreds of thousands of dollars converts couldn't wait to lay at Harold Barnett's feet.

Richard Partridge, the second senior apostle in the quorum, argued that once a tithe or donation had been received, the money became the property of the Lord, and as administrators of the Lord's tithes, they had no obligation to inform the membership how the money was used. The Law of Tithing, he emphasized, was God's law. The responsibility of members was to pay ten percent of their gross annual income and from that point, it was none of their business. He further argued that The Church of Jesus Christ of Latter-day Saints (LDS), the mother church from which they had splintered, handled tithing in the same manner and that is how AJC should handle it.

The AJC official corporate name, The Corporation of the President of the Apostles of Jesus Christ, was only one among hundreds of nascent religious organizations that come and go each year: Harold Barnett as president; Richard Partridge, Registered Agent, and Calvin Barnett, treasurer. The selection of names had been decided upon by the incorporators, the corporate name and bylaws patterned after the LDS Church: The Corporation of the President of the Church of Jesus Christ of Latter-day Saints.

Richard Partridge, a stocky, jowly man resembling an English bulldog with thinning brown hair combed straight back, habitually pressured Harold into adopting more and more LDS-type church functions like Sunday School, a ladies Relief Society and Primary for the children. Before the Black Revelation, Harold insisted that they were strictly a priesthood organization and had no right to usurp the Church. Their calling, he said, was restricted to keeping plural marriage alive and healthy, nothing more. But since the Black Revelation he had to concede that it was the duty of fundamentalists to carry on where the LDS Church left off. Plans were made for an endowment house and bishops were called. On paper, AJC supplanted the LDS Church. The other polygamist groups, drawing the same conclusion, also built their temples and began offering their version of the original endowment.

Since Harold Barnett swung open the doors to new converts wanting to live the "principle" of polygamy, their ranks swelled from a few hundred to what they claimed was now more than 5000, and many of those converts brought with them copious bank accounts, eager to prove their sincerity and loyalty with healthy donations. But the converts were accustomed to participating in church functions and Harold, afraid they would become bored with nothing to do, reasoned that in order to hold them, they should give them more than just plural wives. Patterning after the LDS Church, he divided the priesthood into quorums of Melchizedek and Aaronic. He organized Elders, Seventies, and High Priests, but was careful to place leadership among his and Calvin's sons. Young boys growing up inside the AJC, beginning at age twelve, were ordained into the Aaronic Priesthood as Deacons, Teachers, and Priests. And he rebaptized and reconfirmed each new convert as a member of their mother church, The Church of Jesus Christ of Latter-day Saints. Harold did not recognize AJC as a church. To him there was just one Church, the LDS Church. As the president of the priesthood and presiding elder of AJC, his decisions were absolute and without negotiation. Even though many members of AJC had been excommunicated by the LDS Church, Harold felt he had every right to reconfirm them as members. He saw himself and his followers as loyal, dedicated members in exile.

"The time will come," he predicated, "that a setting in order will come, and during General Conference at Salt Lake City's Temple Square," he assured his followers, "the Lord and Joseph Smith will appear and instruct the LDS Church General Authorities to take seats in the congregation. At that time the Savior will call me and my priesthood to the dais to preside over the Church."

Each of Harold's apostles, according to seniority, was assigned a chair at the conference table. Richard Partridge sat at Harold's left, and Calvin, as the most senior apostle, on his right. If death or incapacitation should remove Harold, Calvin would automatically assume leadership. There could be no deviation because Harold had ordained Calvin as his successor. It was assumed that Richard Partridge would follow Calvin.

Herb Patterson, the youngest of the apostles, at age thirty-six, sat next to Brian Johnson. Marvin Heywood, the sixth most senior member of the quorum, took his seat across from Brian. Parley P. Leatherbury, next in line behind Richard, was on Marvin's right. John Sutton and Brigham Arthur Beal were out of town on assignment. Lazarus Quintana, the fourth most senior apostle and the priesthood representative over the small incorporated Wyoming community of Bitter Creek, seldom traveled to Salt Lake to attend the Sunday morning meeting. Today he was at Bitter Creek, tucked away in a remote canyon forty miles west of Cheyenne. Jesus Salazar, priesthood leader of their AJC Mexican community, located 30 miles southeast of Tijuana, also stayed home. Only during special sessions did they travel the long distance.

Harold called and ordained ten apostles. Their mother church ordained twelve. Officially, he took the position that there were not enough worthy men to fill the apostleship. Unofficially, he had decided that ambitious priesthood men should have this motivation to conduct their lives in such a manner that if called to the apostleship, they would be considered worthy.

In attempts to correct the trend of so many of the children of AJC leaving polygamy, Richard Partridge, Marvin Heywood, Parley P. Leatherbury, and others of the more militant faction of the AJC, pressed for tighter controls. Over time, coercive doctrines were stressed, especially among the women. Dependence upon the priesthood and its infallibility gradually came to be the dominant theme at sacrament meetings. In priesthood meetings, young boys were warned they would be damned if they left the priesthood. In girls' classes, mothers and aunts, in a manner designed to instill fear, inculcated upon the young maidens that a marriage performed by the group priesthood was a girl's only hope to achieve a celestial exaltation, that part of heaven where she could live with God and have her family with her.

Yet, Harold Barnett, supported by his brother, Calvin, persisted with warnings that the people should *rely on prayer* for their answers; he cautioned them not to place confidence in the arm of flesh. Harold reinforced his "free agency dogma" with his favorite metaphor: "Don't expect to get to heaven on the coat sleeves of Joseph Smith or myself. You must make your own way." The more independent, free thinkers in the group perceived the contradiction between Harold and his militant apostles.

The two large oak doors that separated the conference room from the front reception room opened. Harold and the others instinctively looked up. Hilda, Harold's receptionist, secretary, girl-Friday and third wife, asked in her customary all-business voice, "Would you like me to hold all messages until you are through?" Even on Sunday she ran interference for her husband.

As the AJC grew in numbers, members demanded more and more of Harold's attention, especially on Sunday. He was plagued with frequent, mostly frivolous inquires about subjects as diverse as what girl to court and what light bulbs were best.

Hilda lived on the second floor of this old Queen Anne mansion on State Street and seldom ventured out except for groceries. She was as much a fixture in the house as the conference table. Extremely efficient, thin, gray hair coiffured in a bun, gold-framed eyeglasses with sharp Prussian features, she exhibited boundless energy. Partial to long, flowered dresses, of which she possessed many, she exhibited few vices and regulated her life with Germanic resignation. But she did have a fondness for sheer, delicate scarves and was never seen without one around her petite neck.

Three days earlier, an attractive mother of two small children from southern Utah moved in with Hilda temporarily. They occupied the spare bedroom upstairs, next to Hilda. Katherine Sinclair, a new convert to fundamentalism, had been abused by her monogamous husband and hoped to find a new life as a plural wife. Harold and Hilda had been teaching her the gospel from the fundamentalist prospective. Harold was very protective of Katherine, like a father, and knew that because of her beauty she would be sought after by men in his group. He did not want her to go into the wrong family where she would not be treated properly.

Hilda, habitually formal, even when she and Harold were alone, devoted her life to Harold and his business. New customers had no idea that they were husband and wife until they learned that she lived upstairs and every eleven days, so did Harold.

Harold answered, "Yes, thank you, Hilda."

Besides being the leader of one of the largest polygamous groups in the state of Utah, Harold sold insurance and was very good at it. He owed much of his success to Hilda, a tyrant when it came to detail. Many of his customers were fundamentalists, but the majority of his customers resided with the public at large and were active members of the LDS Church. Harold had earned a reputation as a man of undisputed integrity and that overshadowed the prejudice of polygamy. Of his many attributes, his rare ability to keep a confidence reigned highest.

Harold knew he was fortunate to have Hilda. Very few customers insisted on talking to him, those that did were new clients. Ever competent, Hilda knew what forms to fill out, what questions to ask. In her efficient hands, the business had prospered and grown. Harold didn't have to advertize for new customers, it was all he and Hilda could do to handle those who found him by word of mouth. Immensely proud of his business reputation, Harold worked hard to achieve the same perfection in spiritual pursuits and constantly inspired his apostles to conduct their lives as if God himself were watching their every move.

Hilda closed the double oak doors and Harold, habitually attired in suit and tie, asked Parley to open the meeting with a prayer. After the prayer, he asked Marvin to record the minutes, then pulled a white envelope from his coat pocket.

"We have another letter from Phillip Compton," he said, removing the paper with italic typing. He held it up for all to see. "Phillip is getting more nutty by the day. If any of you would like to read the letter, you can, otherwise, I will paraphrase."

His perpetual good-natured visage turned serious and for a moment he looked older than his sixty-four years.

"Phillip thinks he is the One Mighty and Strong and wants to meet with us," Harold said matter-of-factly, no derision or jest in his clear baritone voice.

"Phillip says the Lord has called him to unite all the fundamentalist groups under one head. Naturally, *his* head. He has instructed me to prepare to turn over to him our tithing."

An uneasiness crept across the faces of the apostles. A few squirmed in their seats. Harold continued, "I think he knows our people won't follow him. It's our tithing he wants. He's trying to shake us down just like the mafia. In my opinion, we must take him serious and keep a watchful eye for trouble. Phillip is demented and capable of anything. In the letter, he issued a warning." Harold paused, peering gravely at his apostles. "Phillip states that the rod of destruction is poised to strike all who ignore the Lord's Anointed."

Over the last few years, self-proclaimed prophets claiming to be the One Might and Strong had popped in and out of Salt Lake City making the rounds among fundamentalists, demanding to be recognized. The reference,

One Mighty and Strong, came from Section 85, verse 7 of the Mormon law book, Doctrine & Covenants: "And it shall come to pass that I, the Lord God, will send one mighty and strong, holding the scepter of power in his hand, clothed with light for a covering, whose mouth shall utter words, eternal words; while his bowels shall be a fountain of truth, to set in order the house of God. . . ." The fundamentalists predicted that when the One Mighty and Strong appeared, he would once again return lost doctrines like polygamy to Church members.

Harold and his apostles discussed the mental proclivities of Phillip hoping it would help them know how to respond and what to expect. Marvin, thumbing through his Holy Bible, stated, "Let me read what Isaiah in Chapter 28 has to say about the One Mighty and Strong, and if that doesn't shake you, I don't know what will."

"Woe to the crown of pride, to the drunkards of Ephraim, whose glorious beauty is a fading flower, which are on the head of the fat valleys of them that are overcome with wine! Behold, the Lord hath a mighty and strong one, which as a tempest of hail and a destroying storm, as a flood of mighty waters overflowing, shall cast down to the earth with the hand. The crown of pride, the drunkards of Ephraim, shall be trodden under feet."

Richard Partridge smirked, "If Phillip is the One Mighty and Strong, then I'm King Arthur of Camelot. The guy has lost it."

Calvin retaliated, "Phillip has at least thirty families convinced he is the One Mighty and Strong and they're ready to back him up. I don't think we can take this lightly. He is different from the other crazies going around blowing their trumpet, trying to take over the LDS General Conference every spring and fall."

"Oh he's wacky alright," Brian Johnson inserted, "a dangerous wacky."

The apostles were all well aware of Phillip Compton's demented mentality, bordering that fine line between brilliance and insanity. Two years ago he had splintered away from the AJC apostleship, taking with him a few families. Since then he had picked up more converts culled from other fundamentalist groups, all fanatics like himself. Herb Patterson, the youngest of the AJC apostles, was called to fill Phillip's vacancy.

Intense, tall, lean and bony, with hawkish features and aquiline nose, Phillip Compton's knowledge of the scriptures nearly rivaled the intellect of Marvin, but where Marvin was laid back, Phillip demanded action. Blessed with a photographic memory, Phillip dazzled his acolytes with lengthy quotes from the LDS four standard works—The Holy Bible, The Book of Mormon, Doctrine & Covenants, and Pearl of Great Price. While with the AJC, when it came his turn to preside over sacrament meeting, invariably his arrogance would surface and he'd make it clear that no one could interpret the scriptures like him, and no one could handle money better. He took morbid interest in the doctrine of Blood Atonement and the mission of the Danites, allegedly a secret society of early pioneer assassins. Phillip began conducting unauthorized fireside lessons extolling the exploits of Orrin Porter Rockwell, one of the early Danites, believed to have assassinated several enemies of Joseph Smith and Brigham Young.

"What do you suppose he will do if we don't meet with him?" asked Herb Patterson. Herb remembered Phillip, but hadn't really known him.

"It's hard to tell," said Harold. "He may be bluffing, and again, he may inflict upon us 'a tempest of hail and destroying storm.' He is capable of anything."

Harold adjourned the meeting at 9:30 without deciding what to do about Phillip Compton. The apostles returned to their families in time to prepare for Sunday School that routinely started at 10:30 A.M. Each Sunday morning polygamist families met in homes scattered across the Wasatch Front, that 150 mile stretch of cities along the western slopes of the Wasatch Mountains. The exception was Harold, who held his family Sunday School in the AJC chapel, obscured in an aspen grove at the mouth of Granite Canyon overlooking Salt Lake City. Sometimes as many as 300 men, women, and children worshiped together. After the opening exercises, the children were divided into classes according to age and parent-teachers presented lessons about Jesus and Joseph Smith. The Sunday School format duplicated that of the LDS Church. Harold considered himself and his followers roguish members of the LDS Church. He took the position that they had not abandoned the Church, the Church had abandoned them. He understood that because of political pressures and image, the Church could not accept or welcome them. And when representatives of the Church publicly condemned him for his wayward, polygamist lifestyle, Harold did not retaliate in kind. He firmly believed in the mission of the Church, especially the mission to preach the true gospel to the inhabitants of the earth. He would not be tempted or cajoled into faulting the Church or its leaders. He absorbed each blow of criticism from his antagonists with dignity, and his followers drew strength from his example.

Chapter Three

TWO MONTHS PASSED and Phillip Compton's letter went unanswered. Nothing was heard from him again and he was all but forgotten. A long Indian summer had settled over the region. Although mornings were frosty, the days were still warm. Red and yellow leaves had been stripped from the oak, aspen, and maple trees in the surrounding canyons. Utah was poised for the winter blizzards that would soon swoop in from the northwest. A few puffs of clouds floated in from the western horizon, nothing threatening. Weather-wise, it looked like another beautiful, sunny autumn day.

Industry had slowly pushed out the family homes that once stretched along this portion of State Street until only Harold's two-story, red brick dwelling remained. It was a classic, early Queen Ann structure with a conspicuous onion-roofed tower, two smaller turrets, a decorative porch and encircling veranda. The cornices, soffits, and fancy baroque moldings were all brightly painted, making it an architectural envy among historians. Built before the turn of the century, it had been the home of a miner after he hit the mother lode in the Alta mines. Children pretended it was their castle. Paradoxically, the salient red brick, white filigree trim, and manicured landscape blended harmoniously with the two- and three-story office buildings that dominated both sides of State Street, its conspicuousness provoking intrigue in passers by.

A beige four-door Pontiac cruised past the old red brick house for the second time. The four male occupants stared straight ahead. There was no conversation among them, no looking around, not at the pretty young lady with the short skirt or at the policeman driving by. They especially did not look at the red brick house where an attractive blue and gold sign hung from the white fenced porch—Barnett Insurance Agency.

The Pontiac turned west on a side street near a used car lot and proceeded north on Main Street before it circled back on State Street in a southernly direction, passing the Barnett mansion a third time. The automobile repeated the ritual once more, this time staying in the outside lane. It was 10:10 A.M, traffic was normal, not too busy, but busy enough that a single car with four men would not stand out.

The Pontiac pulled into the driveway and proceeded to the rear of the dwelling that had been turned into a parking lot. There was no other exit. The north and west sides of the parking lot were walled in by office buildings. To the south, behind another office building, separated by a three-foot cement retaining wall, was situated another parking lot containing several automobiles. Behind the mansion, three vehicles were parked in the small lot. The men recognized Harold's maroon Dodge and Calvin's white Ford from the description given them. The third automobile, they identified as Hilda's gray Honda.

The Pontiac turned around and parked in a quick exit position, facing the driveway back out onto State Street. Shielded from view, it could not be seen from the front, only from the neighboring parking lot to the south.

The two men in the back seat and the passenger in the front stepped out. The driver remained in the Pontiac, the motor running. The front passenger, dressed in gray slacks, white shirt, red tie, and charcoal gray sport coat, started toward the back door of the house, followed by the two younger men.

The man in the sport coat, the obvious leader in his mid-twenties, signaled the other two to wait until he tested the back door. The other two were in their late teens. One wore a Navy blue windbreaker over a yellow and brown checked, long-sleeved cotton shirt. The other wore no coat, but was kept warm by a wool, long-sleeved sweater, beige and brown in color, with threaded images of reindeer on the front and back. Both had on blue jeans. Paper-thin rubber surgical gloves covered the hands of all three.

At the signal, the two teenagers climbed onto the wooden porch protected by an iron rod railing. The door was unlocked. The leader cautiously pushed it open and peered inside. Not a word was spoken as they tiptoed inside the spotless kitchen. They hesitated momentarily to get their bearings and listen for any sign that they had been detected.

A white linen table cloth on the kitchen table was bare except for a set of green, apple-shaped salt and pepper shakers and a bud vase filled with artificial daisies. The oak cupboard doors were closed and the drain boards on either side of the empty sink had been cleared of dishes and glasses except for a food blender. A round rag rug lay at the foot of the sink. An odor of cooked bacon still lingered.

To their left, an archway led into a hallway that connected with the front room and front door. Straight ahead, they saw the closed door leading to the conference room. The lay of the rooms matched exactly with the informer's information. They heard the faint sounds of murmured voices from the conference room and a radio playing in the front part of the house.

All three men removed a pistol from their pockets. The man in the sport coat opened the door to the conference room and walked casually inside. Harold and Calvin were seated at their places, papers stretched out in front of them. They both looked up surprised and speechless.

"What. . . ?" Harold said, when he saw the automatic pistol pointed at his face.

What followed only took seconds. The young man in the sweater opened the two oak doors leading to the reception room. Harold was hit in the chest with the first bullet. He barely felt it as he looked at his assassin with disbelief. Three more bullets slammed into his chest, two penetrating his heart. He slumped back, then slid to the floor, his body lodged between the chair and table leg.

The man in the blue windbreaker emptied his revolver into Calvin, who sat frozen and dumfounded. Eight of the shots smashed into his chest, the ninth bullet entered his temple just above the left eye. Blood oozed from the small hole and trickled down his cheek. Calvin's body slouched motionless in the chair. His head suspended grotesquely to one side, the blue sightless eyes staring at the floor, his arms hanging.

Hilda did not notice the doors behind her open, but heard the first shot. She jumped to her feet just as a bullet struck her in the neck, severing an artery. She felt the sting, and warm blood spurted. She made it around the desk before the next bullet slammed into her breast. The bullets kept coming as she fell to the floor, pulling the small radio off the desk. The gunman pumped three more bullets into her back, blood saturating her pink gossamer scarf, puddling on the carpet around her neck.

The three men froze, listening. There was no sound except for the radio on the floor, Frank Sinatra was half way through his rendition of "My Way." The leader, in the sport coat, studied the crumpled bodies of Harold and Calvin—no movement. He then walked into the room where Hilda lay, the automatic pistol still in his right hand. Frank Sinatra finished the last stanza: *"and I bit off more than I could chew."* The leader reached down and clicked off the radio.

The young man in the sweater asked softly, "Should I check upstairs?" The leader looked at him, pondering the question and glanced at the stairway. A motorcycle roared past the house and the three suddenly became aware of traffic sounds outside. "No," he whispered, "let's get out of here," urgency in his voice.

The three men lurched towards the kitchen. "Wait," the leader ordered, "I need to reload." He slid the clip out of the automatic and pulled several long rifle cartridges from his coat pocket, stuffing them in the end of the clip. Then, as an afterthought, he commanded, "Let's pick up the empty shells." The two men immediately scanned the floor, bent and picked at the spent cartridges with their gloved fingers, finding it difficult to pick them up. "There should be ten," said the leader, his voice now more urgent.

"How many you got," he asked, looking at the gunman

with the sweater. He held out his gloved hand displaying five of the small, 3/4 inch empty cartridges.

"I've got four," stammered the gunman with the blue windbreaker.

"We're missing one," the leader cried, the urgency in his voice bordering on panic. They all bent over, twisting and turning, scanning the floor. "It's got to be here!" said the man with the sweater, glancing over at Calvin's body slumped in the chair.

"We can't wait any longer. Let's get out of here," the leader ordered. They all bolted toward the kitchen door in near panic. The leader and the man with the sweater attempted to pass through the door at the same time. The shoulder of the sweatered man jammed up against the door frame, knocking him off balance.

"Hold it, " the leader commanded. "Let's not panic. Walk normal. Follow me."

They hesitated at the back door. The leader opened it a crack, peering outside. The Pontiac was there, the motor running. He pushed open the door just as a car entered the parking lot next door. The car pulled to a stop adjacent to the Pontiac, just beyond the retaining wall. A woman climbed out, walked around to the passenger side, and began unbuckling a child in a car seat. Seconds passed.

"What's the matter?" whispered the man in the windbreaker. "Who's out there?"

"Some woman with a kid just drove up."

The phone rang at Hilda's desk. The two younger men jerked their heads toward the sound as their leader watched the woman stuff something in a pink diaper bag.

The man with the windbreaker placed his hand on the shoulder of the leader and squeezed. "We got to get out of here," he whispered. The telephone continued to ring, a third time, a fourth.

"The woman is taking her damned time," he retaliated.

The relentless ringing continued. The tension and fear in the three men mounted to a dangerous crescendo.

"The hell with it, let's go. Walk, don't run."

The three nervous men stepped onto the porch and down the three steps to the cement. The Pontiac was ten paces away.

The mother, baby in her arms and diaper bag slung over her shoulder, closed the back door of her car as two of the men came around the rear of the Pontiac. Her eyes met the eyes of man in the sport coat. She turned and walked away. The teenagers climbed in behind the driver, and slouched low in the seat.

"We've been seen," the leader said under his breath, griping the handle of the automatic in his coat pocket. "She can identify me, I've got to kill her."

The driver raced the engine and reached over and opened the passenger door. "Come on," he pleaded.

"Come on," the driver cried a second time. But the leader just stood there undecided as the lady with the child walked further away. Aware of watchful eyes, she nervously glanced over her shoulder at him. "Come on," they all pleaded with panic. "Let's get the hell out of here!" The leader jumped in and the Pontiac eased down the driveway, turning south on State Street, disappearing in the traffic.

Jerry Carmichael parked a half block away and hurriedly walked past the several sheriff's patrol cars with their lights flashing red and blue. Deputies rerouted southbound State Street traffic around parked patrol cars. A group of about twenty spectators were gathered just outside the yellow tape cordoning off the crime scene. A uniformed deputy chatted with concerned spectators, attempting to pacify them and keep them out of the crime scene. Jerry recognized two anguished, male onlookers as members of the AJC, and suspected the others were also.

An ambulance blocked the driveway. The center of

activity evolved around a van with the words "Sheriff's Mobile Crime Lab" emblazoned in yellow and brown letters, parked on the lawn beside the ambulance. A steady stream of uniformed and plain clothes deputies wandered back and forth between the van and the mansion. The squaking of a dispatcher resounded in the background, exchanging messages with deputies.

Jerry passed Roy Sutton, the Sheriff's Public Affairs officer who was briefing a cluster of newspaper and television reporters. They nodded recognition of each other. He approached a uniformed deputy at the yellow tape and displayed his credentials. "Inspector Jerry Carmichael, District Attorney's Office, called here by Lieutenant Mike Levine, Detective Division."

The Deputy examined the pictured ID, then said, "Wait here, please," and disappeared in the house. A moment later he returned and motioned for Jerry to step under the tape. "The Lieutenant said for you to meet him in the conference room."

Jerry pinned a duplicate ID to the outside of his suit coat as he walked up the wooden steps of the front porch. Inside the dwelling, homicide detectives had formed into teams of two and were milling around, some holding plastic evidence bags. Hilda's corpse still lay sprawled on the floor. Jerry noticed the pool of brown, coagulated blood around her neck. A photographer snapped pictures of her contorted body from every angle.

Jerry spied Lieutenant Levine through the open double doors. The Lieutenant extended his right hand, "Thanks for coming."

Two other detectives were bent over the twisted body of Harold Barnett. Silver fingerprint dust had been smeared on the oak table and chairs. "You're just in time, as soon as the photographer gets through with the woman in the other room, we're going to turn over the bodies and see what we can find."

Mike Levine was two inches shorter than Jerry's 6' 2", and more stocky. Mike wore a dark gray suit with faint threads of red, a white shirt and clashing red and blue tie. As a homicide investigator, Mike's reputation was well established in the law enforcement community. He and Jerry had participated in numerous law enforcement seminars and both taught at the Utah State Police Academy. Both were graduates of the FBI National Police Academy.

Mike led Jerry over to the corpses and after identifying Harold and Calvin, commenced with his briefing. "We think both were seated at the table when this occurred. We found the kitchen door open and think the shooters, at least two, possibly three, entered by the back door, surprising the victims."

Mike pointed at the kitchen door. "We've been over every square inch of this house and are hurting for physical evidence. All we have so far are a few fibers caught on a tiny splinter of the door jam and one spent .22 cartridge. We don't know if the fibers are related or not. They look like they came from a wool sweater."

Mike's father was Jewish, his mother, Irish. He did not resemble either one but did retain his father's dark, Mediterranean features. Extremely proud of the Jewish side of his family, he'd been to Israel twice. As a youth, before entering law enforcement, impressed over Israel's winning the Yom Kipper War of 1973, he seriously considered emigrating to Israel. Mike's dark, bushy mustache and perpetual beard shadow intensified his handsome face.

"I don't suppose you have any witnesses?" Jerry asked.

Respect between the two men was mutual. Jerry had built his reputation with the Salt Lake City Police Department as an intelligence gatherer and expert on local organized crime. When the District Attorney needed special investigation work, he often drew upon local law enforcement. On several occasions, Jerry had been placed on loan to the District

Attorney to do special investigations. Impressed with Jerry's efficiency, the District Attorney offered him an inspector's slot as head of the urban crime unit. Jerry pounced on the opportunity. Tall and slender, scholastic, natty in apparel and comportment, he stereotyped the role of intelligence officer. Part of his job was to index and profile all the polygamist cults in the State. He had interviewed dozens of dissidents who had lost family fortunes, wives, and daughters to polygamist cults. The losses of most victims, he determined, were induced under the cloak of religion. There was little he could do to help them because, legally, their losses were considered gifts. But he did keep track of who was doing what to whom. So far there had been no violence among the groups. Whenever law enforcement received a complaint about a suspected polygamist, they forwarded the information to the District Attorney. And because the groups and factions were scattered around the State, overlapping into counties and the surrounding states, especially Wyoming and Nevada, it was appropriate to have a central authority that monitored the polygamist subculture. Mike Levine knew that Jerry's knowledge of the polygamist subculture could give him a head start in bringing to justice the people responsible for the cold-blooded murders of the Barnett brothers.

"We have one audio witness," Mike answered. "A woman with two kids, ages five and three. They were upstairs and heard the shooting. Apparently it happened so fast, no one cried out, at least she didn't hear them cry out. When she heard what sounded like popping and realized it was gunfire, she took her kids and hid in a closet."

"Did she hear anything else," Jerry asked, as he watched the two detectives pull the chair away from Harold's corpse and roll him over. The stench of putrid blood, familiar at every murder scene, penetrated the air.

"She heard a young male voice say, 'Should I check upstairs?' and another male voice say, 'No.' I guess she nearly freaked out, pulling clothes off the hangers to cover her and the kids. She stayed that way about fifteen minutes. The telephone kept ringing downstairs. Finally she got up enough nerve to tiptoe down and that's when she saw the woman on the floor. She called 911 and, according to the rookie patrolman that arrived first, she was nearly in a state of hysteria. She's with friends now, we'll interview her again later."

Jerry brushed some fingerprint dust off his gray suit. The detectives found nothing of interest under Harold and moved over to Calvin.

Jerry's short-cropped brown hair was speckled gray around the temples. A Roman nose, enhanced by high cheek bones, gave his handsome features an alertness. Jerry was an active member of The Church of Jesus Christ of Latter-day Saints.

Jerry asked, "What was she doing upstairs, is she one of Harold's wives?"

"Not a wife, a new convert," Mike answered. "She left her abusive husband and was staying with Hilda until she could find a place of her own or shop around for a husband. She's a good looking gal and, in my opinion, doesn't need to share a husband with other women. I asked her, why polygamy? She said she's looking for a good righteous man who will take her to the celestial kingdom and she's convinced polygamy is the only way she can get there."

"Sure," said Jerry sarcastically, "I wonder if she'll feel the same tomorrow morning."

Nothing of importance could be found under Calvin's body, so they moved into the other room where Hilda lay undisturbed. The foul death smell fermented by the puddled blood was even stronger. The gossamer scarf, stiff and blood-glued to the carpet, pulled away with difficulty. There was nothing under Hilda's corpse either. Death is never dignified, Jerry thought.

Mike's cell phone went off; it was the dispatcher. "We have a lady on the phone who says she was next door to the murder scene this morning when she saw three men leave by the back door and get in a car with the motor running."

"Great! Tell her I'll be right over to interview her. Where does she live?"

"There's a problem," said the dispatcher. "She is afraid and doesn't want to get involved. She won't give me her name or phone number. She just wants to know if she can give the information over the phone without revealing her identity."

Mike said, "Trace the call."

"We have, she's at a phone booth on the east side. I've got a car close and he's on the way."

"Look, give her my cell phone and tell her to call me so I can get the information first hand. If she sounds reluctant, keep her on the phone as long as possible. Tell her I will work with her any way I can, but it's imperative I talk with her. In the meantime, have the patrol car keep her under surveillance. Don't let him approach her unless I give the word. Okay?"

Mike looked at Jerry who had already discerned what was happening. "This could be a big break," he said crossing the fingers of his left hand. "Let's go into the kitchen, away from the noise and confusion, in case the witness calls back."

The cell phone wailed while still in Mike's hand. "Lt. Levine," he said in the mouth piece, and then he flashed Jerry the "ok" sign. Mike sat on a kitchen chair, placed his clipboard on the table, pulled out a pen, and prepared to take notes.

The reluctant women said she had an appointment with a realtor next door. As she gathered up her baby girl from her car seat, she noticed three men come out the back door of the red brick house and enter a waiting car. A fourth man sat behind the wheel. She said she might recognize the one wearing a sport jacket who got in the front seat with the driver. She doesn't think she would recognize the other men, but she got the impression that they were all very young, possibly teenagers. Mike said he'd like to show her some pictures, but she said, "No go." She didn't want to get involved, afraid they would come after her, and besides, on second thought, she said she didn't get a good look at the man with the sport coat after all.

Mike did his best, trying to convince her they would give her all the protection she needed. And then she suddenly stopped talking, but did not hang up. "Hello, hello," Mike said into the cell phone. "Are you still there?"

Her voice came back, weak and dejected. "There's a Sheriff's car parked down the street watching me. Did you send him?"

"Yes, I'm sorry. The information you have may save somebody's life."

"And what about my life, you son-of-a-bitch, and the life of my daughter? I wish I had never called."

The phone went silent again but she didn't hang up. Finally, she said, "Okay, I'll meet with you, but if you want my cooperation, you better keep my name out of the papers, and it better stay that way until the trial, if there is a trial." Mike agreed.

A uniformed officer entered the kitchen. "There's a guy outside that wants to talk to whoever is in charge. He says he's one of the apostles of the guy who owns this place."

"What's his name," Mike asked.

"Richard Partridge."

Jerry spoke up. "If I remember right, Partridge is the third senior apostle in the hierarchy and somewhat of a militant and certainly someone we should interview because he is probably now the leader of the group."

After the bodies were transported to the morgue, awaiting autopsies, the red brick mansion was locked and sealed by the

County Attorney until he was confident that all the evidence had been collected. All of Hilda's clothes had to be throughly examined and compared with the fibers found on the kitchen door jam.

Mike's preliminary investigation concentrated on the meticulous task of preserving the crime scene and reconstruction of events. Dozens of photographs were snapped. Finger and palm prints were lifted off the oak table, oak chairs, Hilda's desk, Harold's desk in the same room and anything else that would retain the oily secretions from human hands. The finger and palm prints of each of the victims were taken. Their clothes were removed and sent back to the FBI Fabric and Fiber lab in Washington D.C. The .22 cartridge was sent to ballistics where the mark on the rim made by the firing pin could be photographed for future comparison, in case a suspect weapon was recovered.

The detectives concluded that at least one weapon was an automatic, because of the ejected cartridge found on the floor. Harold's body received ten hits, a clip load, indicating an automatic killed him. Calvin and Hilda took nine hits each indicating nine-shot revolvers were probably used.

The total number of shots fired also helped confirm that there were three shooters, which supported the witness's observation from the adjacent parking lot. Apparently Harold and Calvin had been shot while seated in their chairs. Three .22 slugs were recovered in the oak backrests of both chairs after passing through the bodies. Hilda, they concluded, had been standing when shot. They estimated that the whole scenario, from the time the shooters entered by the back door and climbed back in the waiting automobile, probably occurred in less than three minutes.

Interviews with Richard Partridge and other members at the scene revealed that Harold's followers truly loved him. When they interviewed Brigham Arthur Beal, a humble insignificant looking man, he broke down in tears three times over the loss of his prophet and mentor. Because Beal was more emotionally caught up with Harold, he was less guarded than the others and spoke spontaneously and frankly, volunteering information.

Beal repeated over and over, "I don't know why anyone would want to kill him? He didn't have an enemy in the world." It was from Brigham that they learned of Phillip Compton's letter. They also learned that Harold and Calvin had planned to meet at 10:00 A.M. At first it was assumed that whoever did the shooting was after Harold and killed Calvin and Hilda because they were witnesses. But from what Beal had relayed, they now wondered if the killers wanted both Harold and Calvin out of the way. It also appeared that the killers might have been tipped off as to when Harold and Calvin would be together. That would make Partridge a suspect because he now inherited the leadership.

Chapter Four

JERRY CARMICHAEL met Mike Levine for dinner at the Chinese Ming Restaurant, the local cop hangout, where they dined on pork chow mein while discussing the Barnett murders.

They took a booth at the rear next to the swinging kitchen doors. It was Mike's booth, the establishment reserved it exclusively for him except on rare busy nights when he was elsewhere. Mike was like one of the family. His swarthy presence graced the Ming's doors at least three working nights a week and as many times for lunch. He slid in the booth, facing the front so he could see the cash register and who entered and left.

"Well, we know what happened, now we have to find out why," Mike declared.

"And when we find out why, it's my guess we'll know who," Jerry said casually and then attacked the cup of noodle soup that preceded the chow mein.

An attractive Oriental waitress arrived hefting a large tray with two steaming plates of dried noodles saturated with bean sprouts, celery, chestnut slivers, bits of pork, and a clear, pasty sauce.

"Hey, Lucy, you're all dressed up, you got a hot date?" Crows feet appeared at the corner of his eyes dark eyes as he flashed his million dollar smile. His dark rumpled hair and shadow of beard enhanced the gleam of his ivory teeth.

She gave Mike a playful punch on the shoulder. "Silly, you know this evening work clothes. This high class place."

"Okay, back to business," Mike mumbled as Lucy disappeared in the kitchen. "Tell me about polygamy. What makes them tick? I hear there are 60,000 or more in the western states between Canada and Mexico."

Jerry took a deep breath. "There is a tendency for pseudo-pundits to inflate the number of polygamists, hoping to outrage public opinion and give themselves credibility. A more realistic figure would be 25,000 to 35,000. No one knows exactly." Jerry slurped the last of his soup and with a fork stirred the steaming chow mein.

"Most of them are harmless and present no threat to society. They go out of their way to avoid trouble. In my opinion, most of them are good citizens, they stay to themselves and are careful not to attract attention. Many are well educated. I know of two with doctorate degrees. Their children are often good students and at the top of their class.

"Society doesn't realize it," Jerry continued, "but there is a valid Mormon polygamist subculture out there functioning very well with no signs of dissipating. Like it or not polygamy is here to stay. In the forties and fifties, polygamist communities were raided by the government. More than two dozen men were imprisoned, children were torn from their mothers and placed in foster care. In both cases, nothing was really accomplished except to convey to the world that the LDS Church venomously opposed the practice of plural marriage. The raids were supposed to stamp out polygamy once and for all, but had the opposite effect." Jerry chomped down on a forkfull of chow mein and glanced at Mike who was scooping it in his mouth with chopsticks. Jerry talked while he chewed, Mike was attentive.

"The media highly criticized the government for tearing babies away from mothers. When election time came around, prominent politicians connected with the raids, lost their jobs. Two years later the imprisoned men were out on the streets and reunited with their families. The polygamists then went underground. Today, in numbers, they are stronger than ever, but poorly organized because they can't decide who among them has the sealing keys of authority. The whole idea of 'authority' comes from the doctrine of the LDS Church where they claim that only one man on the earth at any one time holds the keys of authority from God himself."

Jerry explained that in the last few years, as liberalism swept across the country, polygamous cults were viewed by the media as a novelty or nuisance more than a menace. Television networks produced documentaries about the lifestyle and newspapers featured polygamous communities for something to do. "The Plygs, " Jerry said, "were viewed in the same likeness as the Mennonites and Amish except with plural wives, and that is a pretty good assessment. But I think with these murders, that will all change."

While pouring the last of his beer into a glass, Mike asked quizzically, "Are you saying the laws against polygamy don't work?"

"Let me give you an example. According to my informant in the Barnett Group, ten years ago Harold Barnett took a census and counted 150 men with plural wives. Today there are

200 men with more than one wife."

"Those figures don't jive with Partridge's claim that he has 7000 members, unless he's counting family cats, dogs, and horses."

"No, it doesn't," Jerry answered. "It's just another example of exaggerating and inflating figures. I suspect Partridge is trying to look important by making it appear he rules over more people than he actually does. I'm sure he has a few hopeful monogamous men in his group waiting their turn to take plural wives, but they are a small minority and I doubt it all adds up to 7000."

"Okay," Mike asked, "The Barnett Group, or Apostles of Jesus Christ—AJC—is one group. How many other groups are there?"

"There are five main groups. The largest is the Grass Valley Group led by Walt Banks. The AJC is the second largest. There is another group called The Coop that has organized into a form of United Order, which means they have all material things in common. They are primarily economic and agrarian in structure. Where the other groups emphasize authority and scripture, they emphasize thrift and profit. I am told they own dozens of businesses, which includes ranches, farms, and a big gold mine in Nevada.

"The fourth group is much smaller than the other three but is very visual and aggressive. It is run by a dissident from the ATC. The prophet, or so he calls himself, is Phillip Compton. He's the guy that sent Barnett the letter, and my guess, the one behind the murders. Phillip calls his organization, The True Latter-day Church of Christ. He is big on computers and has a website where he does most of his proselyting. My informant tells me Compton is schizophrenic, that he preaches that Jesus Christ visited him and conferred upon him the priesthood keys of authority. To him, that means he has authority over the LDS Church *and* all the fundamentalist groups."

"Maybe you're right and he's our man," Mike suggested. "Is he considered dangerous?"

"Let's put it this way, he is described as a 'fire and brimstone' zealot, and in my book, zealot means he is more unstable than fanatic."

"Then we have a suspect?"

"Well, I would have to say he is capable of murder, especially if he has organized the Danites again. "

"What in hell are Danites, Jerry?"

"Allegedly they were assassins in the 1880s carrying out the law of Blood Atonement."

"Jerry, does this get more complicated?"

"Probably. Blood atonement is a doctrine where a sinner can *involuntarily* atone for his sins by the shedding of his blood. In other words," Jerry said facetiously, "in the early days of the Church, men like Orrin Porter Rockwell, the most famous of the Danites, allegedly saved sinners from going to hell by shedding their blood. The sinner did not choose to die, the decision was made by the Danites."

"You mean they pumped some guy full of lead or cut his throat for his own good? For crying out loud, Jerry, is this what the Mormon Church was all about?"

"I honestly don't know. What I do know is that the Church today is a clean, well managed organization and a great place to raise children."

"Back to our murders," Jerry said. "Granted, we need to take a good look at this Phillip Compton guy, but there is something bothering me that I can't shake. I get the feeling that the shooters knew that Harold and Calvin would be together that morning. I think somebody inside the AJC tipped them off."

"Just one more thing," Mike said sheepishly. "This is a little off the subject, kind'a for my own information. You're a good Mormon, right? I mean, you go to church and all that stuff, right?"

"Right."

"The Church teaches that Joseph Smith and Brigham Young were prophets—in other words, they were the two big guns that got the Church going, right?"

Jerry nodded in the affirmative.

"Both Brigham Young and Joseph Smith practiced polygamy?" Jerry nodded.

"Okay, if I understand this scenario correctly, the Church said it was alright for Smith and Young to practice polygamy, but it isn't now, right?"

"That's about it."

"Amazing." Mike slowly shook his head. "Amazing," he said again. "I read in the paper that there are over ten million Mormons worldwide. Do they know about this blood atonement stuff?"

"Probably not."

Chapter Five

THE ARDUOUS TASK of interviewing the families of Harold and Calvin, and all the AJC apostles, began the next day. It was estimated the interviews would last at least a week, possibly two. So they organized three teams of detectives, delegating to the other teams the lesser apostles and their families. Mike and Jerry selected the most promising interviews, which were Richard Partridge, Katherine Sinclair, and Mary Parkins, the reluctant witness in the parking lot.

It was Mike Levine's case, but in order to avoid confusion to the witnesses and conflict between the detectives, they took turns taking charge of the interviews. Nothing irritated Mike more than to be conducting an interview and have some rookie or idiot detective interrupt his chain of thought with a stupid, leading question. What could be more counter productive, he thought, than two detectives trying to out question the other? Because of Jerry's knowledge of the polygamous lifestyle, he led the interview with Richard Partridge.

A stocky man in his mid-fifties, Richard Partridge appeared to be extremely helpful, more than willing to answer questions about the group organization, which surprised Jerry. Usually you had to drag out of polygamists every tidbit of information. Only where family was concerned did Partridge hesitate, nor would he commit other men on his council to polygamy. His standard reply, "You'll have to ask him that question." Thereafter, they steered away from family questions, especially about wives.

The jowly Richard Partridge, methodical and calculating, took his time answering questions. While he talked, Mike noticed underneath Partridge's white shirt, the outline of the collar and strings of his undergarment. Mike signaled Jerry with his eyebrows, calling attention to the peculiarity. After the interview, Jerry explained to Mike that those Mormons who had been through the temple wore a special priesthood undergarment. The modern garment had been shortened by the Church so it could be worn with short-sleeved shirts and summer shorts. But the fundamentalists still used the old style garment, long sleeves to the wrist and ankle length. The fundamentalists believed the garment to be a sacred pattern revealed by God to Joseph Smith. It has a collar which signified a yoke. Instead of buttons, it was held together down the front by three strings tied in bows. Everything about the garment was priesthood and symbolic.

"The AJC people are known as the *garment people*," Jerry said tongue in cheek, "because they place great emphasis on the garment's importance. As Mike listened to Jerry explain the garment and its purported sacredness, he couldn't help make the comparison in his mind of the witch doctor and the talisman and wondered how intelligent men could go along with such wizardry. And then he reminded himself of the symbology and ceremony in Judaism, the *kipah, talit, tsitsit* and *tefilin,* and kept his thoughts to himself.

Before answering, Richard Partridge weighed each question and its relevance to his agenda as leader of the AJC. If he thought it might help identify the killers without harming his organization, he held nothing back, at least that was the way it appeared. The interview took place in the home of his first wife, Sally. He planted himself in a well-worn, brown leather recliner with his stocking feet propped on a foot stool. His informal and casual demeanor conveyed nothing to hide. He fit the part of a grandfather overseeing his flock, the style unthreatening and believable. However, when questions were sensitive or hit a nerve, his puffy neck and face took on a rosy glow. For the most part, the detectives restricted their questions to the murders. But Mike could not resist venturing into the realm of the "prophet" and after explaining to Partridge, not being a Mormon himself, he was merely attempting to understand the duties of a prophet, Mike asked Partridge if he communicated directly with God?

Partridge squirmed, beat around the bush, mentioned authority, explained abstractly how God works—his response a filigree of innuendos that could be taken any number of ways. The only firm answer was the rosy glow on Partridge's face and neck.

The one thing about Partridge that bothered both Mike and Jerry was that he didn't seem to be as grief-stricken over the death of his leader as the other apostles. It was Jerry's impression that Partridge had welcomed the death of both Harold and Calvin because it meant he inherited the scepter of power in the group.

When speaking about "his people," Partridge feigned the modest, reluctant leader who suddenly finds himself in a position of power—but the smell of arrogance was clear. His words said, "I am a humble servant of God." But very politely and subtly he let it be known that his people were indentured to him and he had complete control over their cooperation in the murder investigation. In his tacit way, he made it perfectly clear that he was giving Mike and Jerry his permission to interview members of his group, including the wives of Harold and Calvin. He said, "Tell me who it is you would like to interview and I will make the arrangements."

Mike shifted uncomfortably in his chair. "Look," he explained. "Do you know how inefficient it will be for us to stop and obtain your permission with each interview. We don't have time for that. Need I remind you that we're trying to find the people who murdered your leader. Why don't you just pass the word that detectives will be conducting interviews and we will try and restrict our questions to the murders."

Jerry enjoyed watching Partridge squirm because he had no alternative now but to cooperate with Mike and he knew it.

Jerry asked Partridge if Harold and Calvin had enemies. He answered, "Harold had enemies. He couldn't help it. Many men have come and gone in our group. Those who leave in anger, or can't live up to our high expectations, blame Harold. Now they will blame me." He smiled, took a deep breath, and straightened up in the chair as if he was up to the challenge. "We are living higher laws and we expect our people to live accordingly. There were occasions when it was necessary for Harold to take away a man's wife because of abuse. This, of course, made Harold the husband's enemy."

Mike thought, this is incredible. This guy thinks he has the authority to give and take another man's wife as if she were his property. And what's even more incredible is that these people let him do it.

Partridge spoke about the fundamentalists in other groups being out of order, that they did not acknowledge the rightful owner of the 'priesthood.' The implication was that it belonged to him. And then with a temerity that staggered both Mike and Jerry, Partridge very carefully and tacitly said, "The leaders in these other groups are not qualified, nor do they have the priesthood authority to seal plural marriages. I take great care and make sure that only those men that are worthy are permitted to take plural wives. Celestial marriage is a sacred covenant. It is not for all men, only those especially called by God."

When Jerry asked Partridge if someone from another group might be a suspect, he hesitated, and said, "I doubt it. I'm not really qualified to give an opinion."

"What about Phillip Compton?"

"He used to be part of our group. I would hate to think he was behind the murders. I rather think it's someone who has lost his wife to our group or had a wife taken away by Harold." He made a big show of how polygamists are hated and threatened by the monogamous families of women converted to polygamy. He said, "It was not unusual for Harold to be threatened by an infuriated husband, brother or father of a converted woman."

Mike asked him, "Are you afraid someone might try and kill you?"

"Not really," he confided. "But as a precaution we are placing guards outside our chapel during meetings. I have several hefty sons watching over me, so I don't worry."

"Who knew that Harold and Calvin were meeting at 10:00 the morning of the shooting?" Mike asked.

"The whole apostolic council. In front of the whole council, Harold and Calvin agreed to meet and go over some prospective real estate documents."

"What real estate documents?"

"It was priesthood business."

Mike's expression darkened and his dander started to rise. Jerry could see Partridge grimace as if he knew what was coming.

"I shouldn't have to drag everything out of you, Mr. Partridge. Are they the same papers we found at the murder scene? Tell me about them."

"A new convert had consecrated a large tract of agricultural land in southern Utah to the priesthood. I doubt that he had anything to do with the murders. His name is Darwin Boston. I'll give you his address."

Mike, astounded, asked the nervous Partridge, "You mean someone donated, free and clear, property to your organization?"

"Yes," he answered matter-of-factly, "we control hundreds of acres of ground that have been consecrated to the Lord."

When the interview was over and the detectives had left Sally's house, Mike said sarcastically, "Jerry, we're in the wrong business. These guys set themselves up with a bootleg religion and suckers can't wait to drop in their laps money and property."

Jerry replied, "Not only that, he's too casual about the danger. It's not normal to be so flippant and unconcerned."

Mary Parkins, an attractive divorcee with a four-month-old baby girl, insisted that her interview be conducted in the office of her attorney, who just happened to be her boyfriend. His name was Clough and according to him, rhymed with tough, and that was the image he attempted to convey.

His office furniture and pictures were inexpensive. He was located in a mediocre building with a bar and delicatessen on the bottom floor, in a mediocre part of town. But there was nothing common or ordinary about Clough, he was an ambitious hot shot attorney. Right off the bat he dazzled Mike and Jerry with an exposition of the high profile cases he had successfully battled, and the huge settlements he had won, leaving no doubt that he was nobody to mess with. His clever use of sophisticated cliches and the prominent names dropped told them he was a man about town. As expected, he clarified in legal terminology that he was holding Mike and Jerry responsible for the safety of his client, who sat beaming by his side, her crossed legs exposed. The unmistakable odor of bourbon and lilac perfume drifted through the room.

"Lt. Levine," Mary Parkins said demurely without the slightest slur, "there is nothing more I can say that I didn't say yesterday on the phone."

"If you wouldn't mind going over it again, possibly you forgot something."

"I didn't forget anything," her words hinting at irritation. "The guy in the sport coat got in the front. The guy in the sweater got in behind him. I can't remember a thing about the third guy, you know, there was a car between us."

Mike and Jerry looked at each other with satisfaction.

"What color was the sweater," Mike asked.

"Tan," she answered without thinking. And then her demeanor softened as though she was surprised that she remembered the color. She stared off into the distance, then volunteered, "It was a long-sleeved sweater and it had a darker design across the chest and sleeves, like bears or deer. Yes, deer heads with antlers."

"Anything else about the man with the sweater?"

"No, I don't think so," she said, still looking off in the distance. "He was young, possibly a teenager. There was something funny about him."

Her attorney boyfriend watched with fascination.

"I know," she said with a smile, "he walked with both hands in his pockets. I thought, how strange. His right hand stayed in his pocket until he climbed in the car. Then I turned away."

Neither detective let on about their excitement. This could be the break they'd hoped for.

"Would you know him again if you saw him?"

"Oh no, all I remember is the sweater. But I would know the one with the blue sport coat. When he opened the car door he looked at me and hesitated for a second and I thought he was going to say something. Then he got in the car and they drove away."

"Describe the fellow with the blue coat."

"In his twenties, short well-groomed brown hair parted on the left. Other than that, he just looked ordinary."

"Any scars, mustache or glasses?"

"No mustache or glasses, but for some reason, I thought his eyes were set closer together than normal."

"Anything else?"

"No," she said, as if relieved of a terrible burden. "Goodness, I'm surprised I remembered that much."

With the tension gone, they went over the descriptions again only in more detail, color of hair, height, weight. Even Clough had softened.

At the end of the interview, she looked deep into Mike's eyes and asked, "Lieutenant, was I any help?"

"A big help," he replied.

"Were they the ones?"

"I won't lie to you," he said as calmly as he could, "we think so."

"Oh!" she gasped. "They know I saw them."

Mike reassured, "I promise your name and testimony will remain confidential until it's time to go to court, if we go to court, then you'll have round-the-clock protection."

Mike gave her one of his cards and wrote his home telephone number on the back. "If you think of anything new or see anything suspicious, call me. If it looks serious, call 911. I don't want to scare you, just be careful and alert. These guys are not professionals. They will want to put as much distance between you and them as they can. If we come up with any pictures, we'll be in touch."

As they stood to leave, Mary thrust out her hand and, with

all the sweetness she could muster, said, "I'm sorry I called you a son-of-bitch on the phone. I was really scared. You don't know how much courage it took for me to call."

Mike shook her hand and said, "I understand. Nothing is going to happen to you and we are going to have those guys behind bars in no time."

As they were driving away, Mike said, "Jerry, you didn't say a word in there."

"Hey, you were on a roll, man. I wasn't about to say something stupid and break the spell. By the way, what do you think made her lighten up. She turned out to be a damned good witness?"

"It was the bourbon," he said, grinning from ear to ear, still elated over the results of the interview. "It gave her confidence and courage and broke down her inhibitions."

Katherine Sinclair had moved in with Margaret Barnett, another of Harold's plural wives. The elderly and obese Margaret, in her reassuring and gentle manner, made the mother and children welcome.

It was the day after the shooting and Jerry's turn to conduct the interview. Margaret said she would entertain the children with books and games in the living room while the detectives interviewed Katherine in the parlor.

Jerry was surprised how calm Katherine appeared. He was also struck by her charm and natural beauty. She wore blue jeans and a cream-colored cashmere sweater. It matched her sandy-colored hair brushed to a high sheen, flowing over her shoulders. Her only makeup was a darkening of the eyebrows and light brushing of blue eye shadow around green eyes. Her full lips were naturally pink and when she smiled, her evenly-spaced white teeth sparkled.

She was younger than Jerry imagined, at least ten years younger than himself, but there was a maturity about her. As she walked into the parlor, her back held straight, her chin high, he concluded that her aristocratic posture was not feigned, but genuine and came naturally. He couldn't help thinking, why does she want to be a polygamist?

He was impressed by the softness but firm grip of her hand. When she sat in the chair next to him, her back still erect, he found himself copying her stately poise, while Mike plunked himself down in slouchy indifference.

She spoke plainly, to the point, and unpretentious. "I will do whatever is necessary to catch those terrible men." The unwavering acoustics of her voice was controlled and pleasant to the ears.

This woman is too good to be true, out of context, Jerry mused and he could see by the look on Mike's face he felt the same way. She had none of the characteristics one associated with polygamist women. No subservient composure. No deference to male superiority. Was she a new breed? There were no signs of lunacy. She was a mystery.

"I heard popping sounds. When I realized they were gunshots, my first impulse was to run downstairs. Then I thought about the children. I whispered, 'let's play a game and see how long we can go without saying a word.' I listened and waited. The children knew something was wrong. It was bad enough their being in a strange house. I tried not to show my fear. When I heard a young male voice say, 'Should I check up stairs?' my heart stopped. That is when I pushed the children in a clothes closet. We crouched in a corner and I pulled clothing down all over us.

"It seemed like hours but was probably only minutes. I could hear Hilda's phone ranging. After about two minutes of waiting and listening, I gathered enough courage to crawl out of the closet and creep down the stairs. I made John and Jill promise they would stay there until I returned."

She's an excellent witness, Jerry thought. Just let her talk. I'll ask her questions when she's through.

"When I reached the bottom steps, I peeked over the

banister into the front room. I froze. I could see Hilda's body laying on the floor. I couldn't believe it. Hilda and I had cooked breakfast together that morning."

She told Jerry it was her first encounter with death. The corpses she had observed in the past had been powdered and groomed, stretched out tranquil in a casket.

"I don't know how long I stood at the bottom of the stairs, looking at Hilda, listening and listening. Once I was sure the killers had gone, I picked up the ringing phone, my hands trembling so hard I could hardly hold it. As I got it to my ear, the caller hung up. I dialed 911. In less than a minute a deputy sheriff came bounding up the front porch. I then noticed John and Jill at the top of the stairs, their faces white as a sheet.

Mike asked, "Will you tell us why you were staying with Hilda?"

In her matter-of-fact way, she said, "I am divorced and was staying temporarily with Hilda until I could find a place of my own."

"You realize that these people are polygamists?"

"Yes, and I may become one myself. I have a sister in the principle, she is married to a wonderful man and is very happy. By comparison, my marriage was a senseless nightmare of jealousy and perpetual abuse. I decided that I would rather have a half, or a third, of a good man, than have all of an immature jerk like my first husband."

Mike, taken aback by her answer and not knowing what else to say, gave Jerry the high sign.

"How will you know what family to go in?" Jerry asked.

"I will know, believe me, I will know, the spirit will tell me," she assured. And then she asked Jerry, "Are you LDS?"

"Yes."

"Do you know that celestial marriage, or eternal marriage, is plural marriage? And that it is the only way we can get in the celestial kingdom."

"I know that's what the fundamentalists believe."

"It's what Joseph Smith and Brigham Young taught and practiced," she countered in her sweet, benign manner. "It is an irrevocable law, and Brigham said, once that law has been revealed to you, you must abide by it or be damned. Something to think about, wouldn't you say?"

John and Jill ran into the room. They were beautiful children, spotlessly clean, modestly dressed and well mannered for their age. The little girl hugged her mother's leg. "Say goodbye to the nice detectives," Katherine gently entreated her. In unison, the children sang, "goodbyeee," the little girl waving her hand.

Mike and Jerry took their usual table at the Chinese Ming. Three uniformed policeman sat in a booth in the corner sipping coffee. The lights were dim except around the oriental lanterns, banzai trees, and the pot-bellied, bronze Buddha beside the check stand.

Mike ordered a plate of Kung Po Chicken. Jerry ordered a combination plate of Moo Goo Gai Pan, Sweet and Sour Pork and Egg Foo Yong. Mike poured his glass full of beer until the foam nearly overflowed.

"You know, Jerry, the husband of that Sinclair dame has to be an idiot to let her get away." Jerry nodded in agreement. "I don't know about this polygamy stuff." he mused. "Could you live polygamy, Jerry?"

"There are a lot of people in the Church who believe someday we will have to go back to polygamy, but I think that's wishful thinking. Even if the government would permit it, I don't believe the women in the Church will ever let it come back."

"Well," Mike interjected, "if polygamy is a priesthood dictum, maybe the women won't have anything to say about it."

"I doubt it," Jerry answered, "the LDS Church is supposed to be male orientated and priesthood controlled, but in many ways the women control the priesthood. The LDS religion is not the all male-ruled, chauvinist church that appears on paper and people think. Make no mistake," he said, "the women in the Church pack a lot of weight."

Chapter Six

THE NEXT MORNING at the daily briefing, Sergeant Morgan approached Mike and said, "There's a guy named Brigham Arthur Beal that you ought to interview. I have him on the phone now. He says he thinks Phillip Compton is behind the killings."

Mike checked his list of AJC apostles. Beal was number eight in the hierarchy and lived in the south end of Salt Lake County. "Tell him to meet me at the Riverton Substation."

Brigham, a mousey little man, fidgeted in his chair. As he contemplated each of Mike's questions, his bushy eyebrows pumped up and down. He said, "If my fellow apostles knew I initiated this meeting, they would accuse me of treason. We're supposed to wait for you to come to us."

"Why?" Mike asked.

"Because law enforcement is still viewed as the enemy. It goes back to the days of the raids in the fifties. We are told not to trust the police, no matter how kind they appear to be. Richard said it is your job to destroy the principle. But I have felt impressed by the spirit to confide to you what I think."

Jerry scrutinized Beal, watching his body language. He was a nervous bundle of humility and sincerity and, although uncomfortable in the role of informer, had gone too far to turn back. Beal said he believed he was fulfilling the will of God, and Jerry thought, maybe he is. In any event, Jerry knew that the little man would reveal to Mike his hidden thoughts, not only about Phillip Compton, but about Richard Partridge, his dictator and leader.

"A month ago, without any warning, Phillip Compton suddenly came to my house and preached to me all one evening. With him were two men he said were his bodyguards."

"What did they look like?"

"One was a big man and the other was smaller but very muscular. Both had beards. Neither said a word and were more interested in what Compton was saying than I was."

They don't fit the description of the shooter, Jerry thought.

"For six agonizing hours I was compelled to listen to Phillip's delusions of grandeur and power. I didn't know what to expect and, honestly, I was afraid for my life. He didn't threaten me or anything like that. He just kept talking about how God destroys his enemies. And then they left as suddenly as they came."

"Did you tell anyone about Compton's visit?"

"The only one I told was Harold, no one else." At the mention of Harold Barnett, the little man sobbed. In between sobs, he confided how he dearly loved Harold and missed him. "I want to help bring Harold's murderers to justice, but I feel so helpless. I prayed and prayed to God and he answered, saying I should tell the police everything and leave the rest in his hands."

From the look on Mike's face, Jerry could tell Mike was wondering if God had really spoken to Beal or if Beal was having delusions of his own. Jerry had never discussed religion with Mike, but knew from subtle remarks that Mike was highly suspect of religion. Nevertheless, as mousey as Brigham Arthur Beal appeared, he had courage, you had to give him that. Religion was his life, and there was no doubt in Jerry's mind that Beal lived his religion as judiciously as he could.

Mike asked Beal if Compton had also talked with other apostles, but he didn't know. But he was sure that Compton wanted both Harold and Calvin out of the way. And then as if spies were lurking nearby, he whispered, "We have a Judas in our midst. As sure as I'm sitting here, someone informed Phillip that Harold and Calvin would be together the morning of the shooting."

"Why?" Mike asked. "What did Compton hope to accomplish by killing Harold and Calvin?"

"I think Phillip killed for two reasons, money and power. He claims to be the One Mighty and Strong and as the One Mighty and Strong, he can command others to give him tithes. I have heard he is deeply in debt and his converts are just as penniless. What money he has been able to squeeze out of converts he has squandered. Under pressure, he becomes more fanatic and outspoken and so he frightens away more people than he converts. I am convinced that the murders are meant as a warning to others. He is after the tithes of all the groups."

Mike and Jerry were fascinated by the intrigue and bizarre beliefs. The intuitive little man continued to frankly reveal in minutes, information that otherwise would have taken days to develop. Both detectives were impressed by his lack of arrogance and guileless casual manner of speaking.

"In order to understand what is taking place, you have to look into the minds of fundamentalist leaders. As I said before, Harold and Calvin's death is a warning to others. He won't admit to killing Harold, but it won't take long for everybody to know he is responsible. Already, the mere mention of his name induces fear. It is rumored that once he brings the fundamentalist leaders to heel, he will target the president of the LDS Church, and then he plans to attack the United States Government."

His whole being took on an ominous countenance that startled Jerry. Looking deep into Mike's eyes, the little man said, "I know this may sound ridiculous to you, but Phillip Compton thinks *he's* ushering in the new millennium."

Unlike his namesake, Brigham Arthur Beal was meek and

unassuming in appearance, but a gargantuan in spirit. In his humble, stammering way, he proved to be a fountain of information.

Beal related how Compton and Richard Partridge were pals before Compton gave up his apostleship and defected from the AJC. When Compton left, Beal said he had expected Richard Partridge to follow, but speculated that because both men were ambitious and dominating, there was room for only one leader. He said that both men were constantly attempting to promote their own agenda. Compton had taken with him about eight families. Brigham estimated their numbers at about 150.

Beal said Phillip Compton settled in the small rural town of Easterdale, Utah. Jerry, who was familiar with Easterdale, said it was situated at the southern most valley of the Iron Creek Mountain Range in central Utah. Easterdale, the detectives learned, was a typical Mormon community. Except for a few maverick coffee drinkers who hung out each morning at the town's only café, Easterdale society revolved around the Church. It was one of those rural towns where everyone knew each other. The local church leaders, for the most part, came from the affluent and prominent families that first settled the area. They were also the same ones elected to the town and county political offices. High school football and basketball, church events, and the movies were Easterdale's prime sources of entertainment.

Brigham Author Beal said that members of Compton's group still communicated with former friends in the Barnett group, and that is how he had been able to keep abreast of what Compton was doing. He said that Easterdale erected a new LDS chapel and, before the city fathers knew what was happening, Compton purchased the old chapel, moved in, and set up shop. His little flock followed, buying up every available house. For two years the old stone chapel became the headquarters of Compton's organization, which he called, True Fundamentalist Church of Christ. Since then the old church has become a beehive of activity.

Beal confirmed much of what Jerry had already learned about Compton and added much more. He gave Jerry a videotape of the man preaching to his congregation, along with two audiotapes of Compton and two of his trusted apostles, all ranting and raving during a sacrament meeting.

Jerry had previously interviewed two dissidents from Compton's group, so he took the earlier statements, Beal's testimony, the tapes, and put together a profile of Phillip Compton.

Compton was an excitable, thin man in his early fifties with boundless energy. He was meticulous in his grooming and sported a mustache and goatee. He had ingeniously indoctrinated his eager flock with newfound self esteem and importance. Most of his followers had been the dregs and culls from other groups. With a strong leader they were able to shelve their inadequacies. Compton was a fearless leader, unafraid of man or beast, and he absorbed his people's fears and became their advocate in seeking recognition and justice. When he spoke, it was with power and conviction. His true believers were uplifted by his audacious forcefulness. For the first time in their lives those impotent dregs were unified with creatures of their own kind and flaunted their artificial assertiveness before the townsfolk, who were cautious not to antagonize them. Deluded with a sense of power, they gorged themselves with Compton's propaganda, strutting around Easterdale confident they were God's chosen people.

Compton, wearing the mantle of a prophet, convinced his hungry followers that they were living all of God's laws and even introduced new laws that further insured his, and their, uniqueness. Before long they worshiped what they perceived was Phillip Compton's ability to crumble mountains and humble kings, presidents, potentates, and even the mighty LDS Church. Phillip Compton became their Savior, the sword of justice that would end years of pent-up frustrations. Soon, Compton promised, their inadequacies would be avenged and the *au fait* powerful, those who build houses high on hillsides where they could be envied, would be reduced to dust. The Church leaders, high powered business men, and smartly dressed politicians with their plush offices in the tall skyscrapers of Salt Lake City, he predicted, would be consumed by the rubble of their crumbling monuments and edifices—when he gave the word.

They did not care that the illusion created by Compton would not occur until sometime in the future. They basked in the symbiotic fantasy as if the imaginary prophecies were about to unfold. Phillip Compton was their prophet, the king over all of Zion, and they were his loyal servants. They believed he had the power of life and death, and as the second millennium approached, Phillip Compton became more vitriolic and descriptive of the apocalypse he prophesied would soon befall the inhabitants of the world. He said it had all been revealed to him in vision, the earthquakes, floods, and geysers shooting hot water high in the sky. He described riots, hunger, and blood flowing in the gutters of Salt Lake, with millions of little yellow soldiers invading from the west.

Jerry telephoned Burt Strong, head of LDS Church Security, while Mike telephoned Sheriff Bud Stewart in central Utah. The Sheriff, half cop, half rancher, had eleven deputies to patrol 5865 square miles and a scattered population of 20,000. Mike briefed the Sheriff, asking if he would assign one of his deputies to make an inventory of all the automobiles in the possession of Compton and his people, particularly a late model beige four-door sedan.

After Mike got off the phone with Sheriff Stewart, he turned to Jerry and asked, "What did Strong think?"

"He said they would beef up security around the First Presidency, which includes the prophet and his top two apostles. He would like us to keep him posted."

It was common knowledge in law enforcement that the LDS Church took fundamentalist activists very seriously. The Church intelligence and security staff was one of the most efficient and well-equipped organizations in the world, equal to that of the Vatican. They recruited heavily from the CIA and FBI and, in turn, the CIA recruited heavily from the pool of returned LDS missionaries because many were bi-lingual and had high moral values. It was a joke in local law enforcement circles that the Salt Lake City FBI Office was more loyal to the LDS Church than to the president of the United States. Many detectives along the Wasatch Front viewed the local FBI Office as little more than an extension of LDS Church Security because of the number of retiring agents in the Salt Lake office that hoped to go to work for the Church.

Each fall and spring, the LDS Church held a three day general conference. Over that weekend, hotels and motels were booked solid with thousands of the faithful coming to attend the semiannual meetings. It was like Mecca twice a year. Temple Square swarmed with eager Mormons from all over the world come to pay their respects to the brethren.

A month before each general session, LDS Church Security hosted a luncheon on the twenty-fourth floor of the Church Office Building in downtown Salt Lake City, where select representatives from all the major local and federal law enforcement agencies issued reports on unstable Mormon dissidents, fanatics, and polygamists in their jurisdiction. Jerry was the District Attorney's representative. Phillip Compton had been high on the Church's list of primary concerns. Jerry suspected that the LDS Security had asked church officials in Easterdale to keep Compton under surveillance.

Jerry asked, "How did it go with Sheriff Stewart?"

"I told the Sheriff we wanted to pay Mr. Compton a visit and would be down his way by noon tomorrow. He said he would meet us at 11:30 A.M. at the local café, the only one in Easterdale."

Mike took out a comb and passed it through his thick dark hair. "Want to catch a bite at the Chinese Ming," he asked.

"I think I'll pass tonight, I have paperwork to catch up on at the office and I promised Beth I would be home early. How long will it take us to drive to Easterdale?"

"I figure four hours," Mike replied. "We need to leave here by 7:00 A.M."

It was 5:30 P.M. when Jerry's office phone rang.

"Inspector, this is Katherine Sinclair. I'm glad I caught you. I didn't want to bother you at home. I have something important I'd like to discuss and I was wondering if you could stop by tomorrow?"

"Is it about the case?" he asked, leaning back in his chair, propping his feet on the desk.

"Yes and no, it's mostly about Richard Partridge and what he is doing to the AJC. People are very concerned."

"Is it something we can discuss over the telephone?" he asked, sensing her anxiety.

"I would rather speak in person if it can be arranged."

"I'm going out of town early in the morning, can we meet tonight?" Jerry had learned a long time ago that when an informant wants to talk, meet with him as soon as possible before he changes his mind.

"Yes," she answered without hesitating.

"Have you eaten?"

"No."

The first place that popped into his mind was the Chinese Ming. But then he remembered the Ming was usually full of cops. They gossiped worse than women.

He said, "There is a steak house near where you're staying called the Balsam Hideaway. I can meet you there in twenty minutes."

"I'll be there."

Jerry pulled a rag from a desk drawer and ran it over his black shoes. In the restroom, he splashed water on his face, combed his hair, smiled for the mirror, and straightened his tie.

She arrived first and was sitting on a fancy bench made of lodge pole pine. A young man and his girl sat next to her, him preening, her giggling. As Jerry walked in he could see she was deep in thought. It gave him a second to study her. It was hard to believe that she was determined to become a polygamist.

When she noticed him, she greeted him with her outstretched hand, and said, "Thank you for coming."

The Balsam was a classy restaurant and she looked right at home, aristocratic and charming. A Jackie Gleason instrumental record played softly in the background, "I Don't Stand a Ghost of a Chance." Jerry wondered why he picked this place to meet. It was far too sophisticated for a professional interview.

The hostess led them to a table obscured in a corner where a lighted candle in a blue indigo, antique bottle flickered. Jerry couldn't help notice the glances of several male patrons as they threaded through the tables.

Katherine began the conversation. "People in the group are talking. They are worried about Richard," she said. "He is doing exactly what Harold refused to do. I guess it is no surprise. While Harold was alive, I'm told Richard pushed and pushed to get his way, and now, before poor Harold's body is buried, Richard has become a law unto himself."

"What exactly is he doing?"

"He claims that the LDS Church has lost its right to hold the keys of the priesthood because they have abandoned celestial marriage, the united order, and law of consecration. He claims *he* now holds all the keys of the priesthood because, as he puts it, 'we are the only people on earth living all of God's laws.' He is teaching that God will sustain him because of who he is. I am told he is sounding like Phillip Compton."

"Jerry, Richard has turned himself into a surrogate God. He is telling certain people that no one can gain access to the celestial kingdom or meet Jesus Christ *except through him.* He calls it The Law of Introduction."

"That's something I haven't heard before," Jerry replied. "How are the people reacting?"

"Half the people believe him and the other half are going along because they think he holds the keys."

A waitress in the costume of an Austrian mountain climber stood over them. They both ordered prime rib, Jerry asked for an end cut.

"Richard thinks he will take over the LDS Church. The man's arrogance is horrid, he says he'll continue to permit the Church to send missionaries throughout the world because it fulfills prophecy. Can you believe it. And then he said he will gather from the orthodox membership, the elite, the true believers—the *creme de la creme*—as he calls them."

Jerry didn't tell her he had already been informed of most of what Partridge was doing. The fact that she was upset, he thought, was a good sign. Very possibly it might change her mind about becoming a polygamist.

"Harold would never have permitted this. Those close to Harold, his wives and his children, are very upset. Some of them are talking about leaving the group. Others don't know what to do. Their social lives revolve around the group, their friends, their families. They don't know where else to go, because they believe the keys of the priesthood are in the group. Jerry, these are good people who just want to live their religion, earn a living, and conduct their lives unmolested. They are no threat to anyone. But they are afraid Richard's going to bring them unwanted attention, resulting in persecutions from the Church and the law. I too would go somewhere else, but I have a testimony that the keys for the eternal sealing of plural marriages is with this group."

Her last statement about priesthood keys turned him off. How on earth, he thought, could she even think such a thing?

"Why would the Church persecute them?" he asked.

"All polygamists believe that in the forties and fifties, when the government raided the polygamist communities, that Church officials were behind it. Polygamy is a perpetual embarrassment to the Church."

She sipped from the tinted water glass. "Jerry, we all know the Church is the most powerful organization in the State of Utah. Their prestige extends from one end of the State to the other and around the world. They influence legislation, law enforcement, the courts, and city governments."

"I can't dispute they are influential," Jerry agreed. "But power is the name of the game in this world. Most members are proud of the Church's influence and connections with government. You see, in the early 1900s, when the railroads established themselves in northern Utah, non-Mormons swooped down on Salt Lake City and captured control of city government. For over twenty years, Salt Lake City boasted a red light district as notorious as Reno, Nevada, and San Diego. Brothels, saloons, and tobacco shops on Commercial Street slopped over onto State Street under the very shadow of the Temple and LDS Church headquarters. The brethren were patient and bided their time. Slowly, under the economic tutelage of men like Heber C. Grant, who as you know was the eighth president of the Church, they climbed back into the seat of government."

Katherine then confided to Jerry that Richard Partridge had let it be known that he was interested in her as a plural wife. An image of the jowly-faced Partridge popped into Jerry's mind and he cringed with disgust.

She said that Partridge had pulled her aside that very morning and whispered in her ear that the Lord would be very pleased if she were to come into his family. There was no mistaking his intentions. His remarks forced her to face the possibility that in matters of matrimony, the Lord might expect her to obey a priesthood edict. It created a serious dilemma. The physical features of Richard were repulsive to Katherine. What should she do? He was now in a position of supreme authority with the right to approve or disapprove any marriage within the group. If he were to say that the Lord wanted her to marry him, his word was considered as good as the Lord's. Down deep she knew that she must do what the Lord asked her, obedience took priority over personal feelings.

And then she revealed that Parley P. Leatherbury had also made overtures towards matrimony. But the spirit, she said, had not given her a witness of either Partridge or Leatherbury. She was not attracted to either man.

She disclosed to Jerry that when she first met Harold Barnett, in his fatherly way, he had told her to take her time and not rush into a marriage. She indicated that she had complete confidence in Harold. But now, without his wisdom to fall back on, she had come to Jerry for advice. "I'm sorry to burden you with my problems," she told him. "I needed someone who not only understood my problem, but was removed from the group and could be objective. If I only had time, I know I could work this all out."

Jerry knew better than to allow himself to become emotionally involved in an investigation, especially with a witness. But he couldn't stand idly by and let her marry Partridge or Leatherbury without doing something. It would be easy for him to say to Katherine—Those guys are creeps and phoneys, all they want is your body and the prestige of your beauty.

Instead he found himself telling her about Beth, her virtues as a wife, her compassion for others, her dedication and work in the ward relief society and how much alike they were, she and Beth.

"She sounds like an exceptional person, I would like to meet her."

He responded immediately as if he had been taken of the hook, "Good, how about dinner, day after tomorrow? We can meet here. You will like Beth, she is much better at things like this than I am.

"You have to understand," he cautioned, "that I don't believe Richard Partridge has any *keys* or has the right to tell you God has picked you for his wife. Beth is very understanding, and you're right about seeking advice from someone unrelated to your problem."

She looked at him quizzically. "You're very kind."

But then it occurred to him that by putting her off a full day before meeting Beth, she might change her mind. So he explained to her again that tomorrow he and Mike were driving to Easterdale to interview Phillip Compton, and he did not know how late they would return; otherwise, he would introduce her to Beth tomorrow night. She agreed that the interview with Compton was more important and wished him well, cautioning him to be careful. She appraised him of the gossip circulating in the group about Phillip Compton.

Jerry asked, "Who on the council is close to Phillip?"

"I don't know, but I can find out. Harold's murder has resulted in more speculation and gossip than you can imagine. There is one thing I have learned about fundamentalists," she confided. "They pride themselves on being well informed. Gossip is an important part of their everyday lives. I have noticed that there are three women in the group, wives of apostles, who pretend to know everything that is happening. They have an answer to every question and, because they are married to apostles, are very much respected by other women, and many men, especially new converts. These women are very popular as sources of information."

Jerry listened attentively, fascinated by what she was saying. In the next few days, as more and more information was gathered, he would come to realize that in the Barnett group there was a strong matriarchal hierarchy.

Katherine said, "It is commonly thought that polygamist women are oppressed by the men. That is not entirely true, at least in the Barnett Group. Women in the AJC have their free agency and are very active in converting other women. I was converted by my sister. It was she who introduced me to Harold. At first, Harold attempted to persuade me to remain in the LDS Church. I had to convince him that I was ready for a life of polygamy. He said the Church teaches that polygamy is no longer necessary, that a monogamous temple marriage will do the same thing, that a husband and wife can be together in the next life, *and* can procreate there."

"Do the women in the other fundamentalist groups have as much freedom as you?"

"I'm afraid not. As you probably know, the Grass Valley group is a closed society and ultra conservative. When they settled Grass Valley in the thirties, the women dressed in the fashions of the day. The rest of the world changed but they didn't. They still do their hair the same way and wear long, homespun dresses. In Grass Valley when a young girl physically matures and can make babies, she is expected to present herself before the priesthood for placement in a family. Unfortunately, there have been times when fourteen- and fifteen-year-old girls have been placed with much older men, sometimes with men old enough to be their grandfathers. The priesthood controls who they marry and when. That is not how it is supposed to work. Women in closed societies like Grass Valley have very little free agency."

"But you said Richard Partridge would have to approve your marriage, isn't that the same thing"

"Not really. The AJC priesthood does not arrange marriages, it just approves marriages. It is the woman who often initiates the relationship. She finds a family where she feels compatible, gets the approval of the wives, and then they all approach the husband. If he can financially care for another wife then he is obligated. If all is well, they go to the priesthood for approval. Of course, it is not always that simple." She smiled. "Economics are important. The husband must be able to afford another wife. All too often, couples are so anxious to marry that these things are not considered. But, for me, the most important aspect of going into plural marriage is compatibility with the other wives. If the wives are unable to get along, my sister said, it is hell for everyone, including the husband. That's why in many cases, the wives go out recruiting new wives."

"It sounds like you have studied this out very well. I had heard that current wives must approve new wives, but I didn't know wives were permitted to look for new wives."

"In the Barnett Group, thanks to Harold, the women have much more freedom. From what I've heard, wives recruiting new wives is not a common occurrence in the other groups. Of course there are jerks in the Barnett Group, guys who think that while married to one woman they can go around dating other women pretendong they are single. Some have been known to go to LDS Church social dances, again pretending they are single. They find some cute girl, she falls in love with him, and then he converts her to polygamy."

Furrows appeared between her eyes, and she thumped the table with an index finger. "And then there are the men who pretend they have received revelation that some girl belongs in their family. These are the incidents that demonize plural marriage. In most cases, the assimilation of women into a family is as smooth and natural as in monogamy."

Katherine did not try to skirt around the negative aspects of polygamy. She acknowledged that the Grass Valley people were out of order. She quoted from Joseph Smith who said, "When a man abuses his authority, amen to that man's priesthood." Nevertheless, she still insisted that plural marriage was a correct principle.

Katherine was unlike the other women Jerry had seen in the AJC, resigned to their obscure circumstance, submissive to priesthood, stagnating in a ghetto-like mentality, culturally and spiritually dependent upon a central authority figure. In every respect Katherine was monogamous, except for the issue of authority. The nightmare of her previous marriage, he guessed, had caused her to place all of her trust in a religious doctrine.

Chapter Seven

THE HIGHWAY WEAVED around sagebrush and cedar-choked hills, dipping into arid valleys where cattle grazed and jack rabbits raced across the highway. With Mike at the wheel, they reached Easterdale in three and one-half hours. They stopped twice, once for coffee in the old mining town of Eureka, and a second time to read the plaque on a stone monument where the highway intersected the famous Pony Express Trail.

Commerce in Easterdale was basic and agrarian, meant to service the everyday needs of its customers. The prominent buildings of the town were the high school and new LDS Church. Service stations were located at each end of town. The highway was Easterdale's main street. On it could be found a bank, post office, town hall, country grocery store, hardware store, farm implement sales and service, a fast food drive-in, and the social center of all gossip and secular activity—the local café. Most of the houses were older and dated back to the forties or turn of the century. English, Greek, and Danish influence were evident in the architecture, with Gothic designs, popular among the English immigrants who settled the area.

An antiquated neon sign flashed in faded red script, "Mom's Homemade Dinners." In the parking lot, sheep dogs patiently lounged in the beds of parked pickup trucks. One rusty pickup was laden with baled hay. The only automobile was a white, mud-splattered Ford with a gold star painted on the front doors.

Inside, a large picture of John Wayne surrounded by a sand painting of Indian petroglyphs adorned the wall. The dining room was a circle of booths with eight tables in the center. Mike and Jerry were the only two men in town wearing suits and ties and, when they sat opposite the Sheriff in a back booth, they became the object of attention. The café was half filled with whispering, country clad diners that eyeballed the two detectives.

Sheriff Bud Stewart was dressed in a short-sleeved, forest green shirt, open at the neck, with yellow "Sheriff" arm patches. A sweat-stained, open-road Stetson was tipped jauntily back on his head, exposing a lock of thick black hair that fell over his forehead. The rest of him was faded Levis, cowboy boots with horse manure stuck to the soles, strong calloused hands, and a weathered face. He had obviously spent more time out in the fields than behind a desk.

After the introductions, Mike asked the Sheriff if he had any luck locating the beige four-door sedan. A freckle-faced waitress took their order.

"Call me Bud," the Sheriff ordered, "we're not much on formalities around here. My deputy tells me he has seen a beige car parked at their church house on one or two occasions, but he can't find it now. Possibly it's hid out in a garage, barn or stashed up in the hills."

"Do you know if Compton is in town?" Jerry asked.

"Yep," Bud replied. "His maroon Ford is parked in front of the church. He spent last night with his favorite wife, Claudia, who lives just up the street."

The Sheriff named off Compton's ruling hierarchy. They were men of varying ages, from their early twenties to their mid-seventies. He plucked a photograph out of a 9 x 12 brown envelope and slid it across the table. "This is a group picture of Compton and his entourage. It was taken on Labor Day at one of their picnics. He doesn't know I have it."

The Sheriff took a red ink pen and made a dot over the head of a smiling slender man with a goatee. "This is Phillip Compton."

The two detectives scanned the photograph. There were fifteen men in all. Only three of the group were clean shaven. They looked for a young man with narrow eyes. None fit the description.

Most of the beards were Brigham Young style, full, well combed with no mustache. The Sheriff placed a red dot over the head of a tall, burly, bearded man in his forties.

"This guy is Buck Jones, the most militant of his ruling council. They say he's strong as a bull. The stocky, well built guy on Compton's left is Karras. I've never heard a first name. He and Jones are Compton's bodyguards. Watch out for them." Bud put a red dot over his head.

"When Compton wants to make an impression, he pretends his life is in danger and has Mutt and Jeff tag along for effect." He placed dots over two other bearded men. "These fellows," he said, making an x over each man, "are his soldiers."

A deputy sauntered in and sat next to the Sheriff. He was a little older, graying around the temples. "Bud," he said, "my informant thinks a kid named Douglas Cooper has a beige four-door sedan, a Pontiac, but he hasn't seen it for a few days. I ran his name on the computer—no record."

"Tomorrow we'll pick up a copy of his driver's license picture from the State," Mike interjected.

Mike summarized Mary Parkins' descriptions of the shooters. The narrow eyes of the man in the blue sport coat, the sweater, and the beige vehicle were all they had to go on, but neither the Sheriff nor the deputy could remember seeing one of Compton's men with conspicuously narrow eyes.

"Maybe Mary only thought he had narrow eyes," Mike lamented.

The deputy left. Sheriff Bud Stewart folded a dollar bill in half and set it on the table for a tip. Jerry pulled out his wallet, but the Sheriff motioned for him to put it away. "Drinks are on the house."

Jerry asked, "How do the locals feel about Compton and his gang of fanatics?"

Bud paused, collecting his thoughts. "To begin with, everyone is angry at the realtor who sold him the old church house." He laughed. "Naturally, they wish Compton would go away, but they know he has as much right to live here as anyone else. A few have pressured me to arrest him for polygamy, but you know what a mess that would be. They would have me looking into bedroom windows, following everybody around. I haven't got time for that and it ain't going to solve anything. There have been polygamist families living in these parts for years and they haven't caused anybody any trouble. But this Compton guy is different. He tries to stir up the old established polygamist families. But they don't want no truck with him. The people he's sucked into his group are all new to us. I don't know where they're coming from."

Bud Stewart leaned back in the seat like he was Will Rogers about to spin a big yarn. "You know how standoffish people are in a small town, a phobic-fear of foreigners and all that? Six months ago reporters and television crews from England converged on Easterdale filling up the motel with cameras and microphones. This was a time when, you know, polygamist cults were portrayed by the media as harmless novelties. Compton attempted to capitalize on the media exposure by characterizing himself as a harmless old country sage, a man of God whose sole intent is to organize a communal lifestyle. He mixes into his talk innuendos like 'praise the Lord' and 'thank God,' to give himself credibility.

"For a while the strategy works and out of a dozen or more new converts, three elderly couples were induced into selling their houses and turning the money over to Compton. I figure this netted him around $750,000, tax free."

Mike and Jerry, impressed with the background information accumulated by the Sheriff, listened in amazement. They learned that Compton targeted older people, especially those with health problems, hoping they would soon die. The Sheriff continued sarcastically, "He convinced the old people that he could guarantee a celestial exaltation if they would consecrate to the Lord their time, talent, and assets, withholding nothing, just like it says in the Temple Endowment. If they balk, he shames them with the Biblical accounts of Ananias and Sapphira, who held back part of their tithes and were struck dead."

The Sheriff revealed that Compton invested his money poorly and spent liberally, especially on himself. At one time he had enough money to pay off the old stone church. But what he did was put down just enough money to move in, and blew the rest. Now he was having a hard time making the large payments. He was so impressed with his ability to convert new people that he thought there would be a steady flow of wealthy converts to make ends meet. It didn't happen.

The Sheriff said some of the money went towards remodeling the inside of the chapel. Half of the chapel was converted into a temple and endowment house, and the other half into an assembly hall, large kitchen, five classrooms, a conference room, a television room, a computer room, a private office, and three bedrooms. The basement was used to store food, water, blankets, building tools, candles, first aid supplies, guns and ammunition—everything they would need to protect and sustain themselves over a prolonged stay.

After Compton swindled the life savings from two

families, he excommunicated them when they started asking questions about how their money was used. "It's the Lord's money now and none of your business," he told them. Compton insisted upon absolute obedience. He would not tolerate any degree of insubordination.

The old stone chapel was U-shaped, consisting of two huge wings joined in the middle by a large hallway, with classrooms towards the rear. It was located on a corner one block east of the main street. The stone walls were made of rough-cut granite, quarried from nearby mountains. Wood shingles on the roof glistened from a recent oiling. The lawn in front was well kept. There were several parked cars in an asphalt parking lot at the rear, one had a flat tire. Following the Sheriff's instructions, Mike and Jerry entered by the side door of the south wing. They were immediately met in the hall by a comely young woman in a long dress. Mike flashed his ID and badge, and explained they would like to visit with Phillip Compton. She asked them to wait while she checked to see if Compton would see them. She disappeared down the hall.

Several minutes passed. A young man approached them from the assembly hall, passed them without speaking and went outside. Seconds later he came back inside, glanced as he passed, and entered the room where the young woman disappeared. Mike says, "It's my guess the kid is checking to see if we are alone."

The young woman returned. "Mr. Compton will see you in the conference room," and she led them down the hall.

Inside the conference room was a cafeteria table and a dozen folding chairs. The walls were bare. A window with the curtain pulled shut faced west. The room was situated between the two wings of the church. A thick book was positioned in the middle of the table. It was the Mormon standard works—a combination book containing the Holy

Bible, The Book of Mormon, Doctrine & Covenants, and Pearl of Great Price.

They sat down facing the door, their backs to the windows. Minutes more passed. Mike rolled his eyes. They were about to go back out in the hall when the door burst open and in walked the bearded, scowling Buck Jones, looking about the room menacingly as if there might be more in the room than the two detectives. Karris followed. The two startled detectives, recognizing Jones from the Sheriff's picture, jumped to their feet, hands dropping instinctively to the sidearms under their coats.

Jones put his hands up chest high showing he was unarmed, motioning them to sit down. His open hands were the size of hams and he towered over Jerry by at least four inches. His forehead was wrinkled, crows feet stretching horizontally from his eyes to his hair line, brown hair combed straight back. He wore a plaid long-sleeved shirt. His deep voice boomed, "Who are you and what do you want?"

Karris stood next to Jones, hands on hips in a combative posture. He had massive shoulders for his size, indicating he had spent many hours lifting weights. He too wore a plaid shirt, open at the neck, exposing brown chest hair that merged with his beard. His hair was also combed straight back. Mike told himself, they must have the same barber.

Still standing, Mike slowly reached inside his coat pocket, retrieving the leather folder with his badge and ID. Jerry did the same. Jones held them close to his face, examining them carefully, then handed them to Karris.

Mike spoke first. "We want to talk with Phillip Compton," It was more command than request. He would not be intimidated.

Karris contemptuously tossed the ID folders on the table. "What about?" Jones challenged.

"About the murders of Harold and Calvin Barnett. We understand Mr. Compton was once associated with the

Barnetts. We believe he might help us identify the people responsible."

Jones' eyes glared with defiance "Do you think he had anything to do with it?"

"We don't know at this point who did it, we are talking with everyone who knew the Barnetts. We're looking for help."

A smirk formed on Jones' face. "I want your guns before you talk," he commanded, holding out a massive right hand.

"You know better than that," Mike replied with disgust. "We don't give up our weapons. Compton is in no danger from us. Do we see him or not?"

Jones stared down at Mike. Neither budged. Jerry watched Karris out of the corner of his eyes, ready for whatever came next.

Finally Jones said, "Wait here," and went out the door. Karris stood firm, his arms folded.

Mike decided to do a little intimidation of his own and faced Karris demanding, "What's your name?"

He hesitated. "Karris," he finally replied as if it were a name that should strike fear.

"Nice place you got here," Jerry interjected, hoping to break the tension.

"It's a beginning."

Mike rolled his eyes.

The door opened. Jones entered followed by Phillip Compton wearing the expression of a busy man who has been untimely interrupted. Just like his picture, not a hair out of place. His build was slender. He was the same height as Jerry. He sat while Jones and Karris remained standing behind him like gargoyles. "Now what can I do for you gentlemen."

The two detectives sat. Mike spoke first. "We are investigating the murder of Harold and Calvin Barnett. We were wondering if you could help us locate the people responsible?"

"Why do you think I can help? I haven't seen Harold for over two years. And what makes you think I would want to help?"

Mike could see that the interview wasn't going to go anywhere. Disgusted and knowing that he was about to lose patience, he gave Jerry the high sign to assume the interview.

Jerry said, "Wouldn't you like to see the people responsible caught?"

Compton looked into Jerry's eyes and assumed the demeanor of a fortune teller. "I am able to discern the spirit of you two men. I knew what you were as soon as I entered the room. You're not fooling anybody. You're here to play mind games. I know you met with the Sheriff before coming over here. I'm not stupid. I know you would like to pin those murders on me. You are working for the LDS Church. You want me out of the way."

"It's not that way at all—"

Compton rudely cut Jerry off, raising his voice. "The brethren in the LDS Church want me dead because they know they are out of order and that I hold the keys now. I know what they are saying about me. They call me the little mafia, but it is they who are the mafia, the real Mormon mafia. I know how they work. They use their power to corrupt and coerce little guys into doing what they want. I have talked to their victims and I have seen in visions their plan to dominate the planet. They have strayed from the plan of God and have established their own God, which is money and power. They are a nest of vipers in league with the Illuminati and the Jewish priests who sacrifice babies to their god, Satan."

Mike and Jerry listened to his diatribe without saying a word. Even with advance knowledge about Compton, they were dumfounded. They watched as he worked himself into a trembling rage.

"Who are you two men?" He suddenly stood up, looking down at them, his face flushed. They stood, facing him.

"Mike and Jerry? You gave me phony names. You're nothing but cartoon characters, instruments in the hands of the LDS Church, playing your evil mind games. Do you have a warrant for my arrest?" he demanded, glaring at Mike.

"You know we don't."

Half shouting, still trembling, his voice an octave higher, "Then get out of my church and don't come back without a warrant, and if you do come back, you better bring lots of help!"

Buck Jones towered, arms folded, half blocking the doorway. They had to turn sideways to get past him. Jerry went first. Mike hesitated in front of Karris. He reached into his coat pocket, removed a skull cap with the Star of David embroidered on the top and placed it on his head. Nose to nose with Karris, he said menacingly, "Did you know I was a Jew?"

Karris was momentarily stunned, his mouth agape, but didn't flinch. Recovering, his upper lip curled revealing yellow-stained teeth.

"Come on, Mike," Jerry urged.

Pretending reluctance, Mike followed. Halfway down the hall Mike stopped and turned. Compton and his two henchman were standing beside the conference room door, watching. Impulsively, Mike made a great sweeping bow with his right hand. "Have a nice day, gentlemen." He then meandered mockingly the rest of the way down the hall as if he didn't have a care in the world.

Jerry held the door open for Mike and whispered, "Are you nuts? Those two gorillas could have eaten us alive."

"Jerry," he answered, "there is one thing I learned about being Jewish. Never show fear. Besides, I couldn't resist, the devil made me do it."

They met Bud Stewart in his office at the City Hall, a plain, rectangular brick building with a flagpole on the front lawn.

The Sheriff was hanging up the telephone as they walked in. Laughing, he regained his composure, and said, "That was Compton. He said you guys are playing mind games with him and he wants me to run you out of town."

They informed the Sheriff what happened and after discussing Compton's paranoia, they all suspected that Compton would like to be pushed into a confrontation like Ruby Ridge where he could elicit national attention to feed his quenchless ego. Before starting back to Salt Lake, the city detectives slowly cruised past each house that was known to belong to one of Compton's members, knowing they would be seen. Compton had accused them of playing mind games, they didn't want to disappoint him.

Ten minutes out of town Mike's cell phone rang. Mike listened to the caller on the other end, his face turned stony, and then he said to the caller, "Damn! I'll contact you as soon as I get back."

Jerry braced for the bad news. "They found Brigham Arthur Beal dead in his front doorway, his throat cut. One of his wives found him. They think he's been dead an hour."

They met Sgt. Moeller at the morgue. A doctor and Moeller had just removed the clothes from Beal's corpse and were examining the body for marks and clues. The only pertinent mark was a laceration on the back of his head where he had been hit with a blunt instrument resembling a pipe. In reconstructing the killing, Moeller surmised that Brigham had attempted to flee into his house when he was struck from behind. The doctor suspected the force of the blow was sufficient to fracture the skull and cause death, but he would reserve judgement until after the autopsy. It appeared that Beal fell face down and then rolled over. Moeller said he was probably unconscious when his throat was slit from ear to ear, clear to the spinal cord.

Mike said, "The poor little bugger. Whoever done the job went to extra effort, a little further and Brigham would have been decapitated."

Mike asked Moeller where Beal's three wives were at the time of the murder. He said they had gone to a relief society meeting and had taken all the children with them. Mike shrugged his shoulders, looked down at the naked corpse, "Not much to go on. No witnesses, no knife, and no blunt instrument. All we have is a motive. I think it's quite obvious the gutsy little guy found the Judas, and the Judas killed him."

News of the little man's death spread quickly through the Barnett Group. Richard Partridge, looking for Mike, personally contacted Sgt. Moeller offering his help. In the course of the conversation, he let it be known that he and Marvin Heywood had just left a fireside where both had been speakers about the time Beal was murdered.

In checking out Partridge's story, Sgt. Moeller said that Partridge and Heywood could have left the fireside, driven to Beal's house, cut his throat, gone on to Heywood's house and still been within the time frame. Moeller assigned two detectives to interview Heywood's wives. They confirmed that Partridge had come into the house and stayed for at least an hour while he and Heywood discussed the scriptures.

The next morning Mike and Jerry met with Partridge and his council of apostles at their meetinghouse in the mouth of Granite Canyon. They were all there except Jesus Salazar who was in Mexico. Lazarus Quintana, the apostle in charge of their southern Utah ranch, happened to be in Salt Lake on business and attended the meeting.

The meetinghouse was a large frame structure, basically an auditorium, a stage, and podium at the east end. Classrooms lined the north wall. The building was used for Sunday spiritual meetings, banquets, and dances. Basketball hoops were fastened on backboards that could be lowered into place.

It was located in a wooded area of oak brush and aspen trees. Several tall ponderosa, planted many years prior, marked the new quarter-mile asphalt road that led from the main canyon road. The property was used as a picnic and camping area by the group until the meetinghouse was built. A large 200 car parking lot had been cleared of brush on the south side. Overlooking the Salt Lake Valley, it was an ideal location, unpretentious, obscured from the busy roadway leading up the canyon to the ski resorts.

The mood inside the conference room sobered abruptly when Partridge entered. The apostles were patient as Partridge shuffled around papers. They waited in deferential protocol for him to make the introductions and officially take charge.

Partridge's little ego ritual perturbed Mike. Out of the corner of his eyes, Jerry studied the demeanor of the apostles. Some were glassy-eyed with awe. The rest sat quietly, their eyes on Partridge. A couple found time to clean their fingernails with small pocket knives.

Mike did not wait for Partridge to complete his ego ritual. Sounding very official, he stood and said, "Gentlemen!" The astonished eyes of the apostles shifted quickly to Mike. Partridge's head snapped up, a mixture of surprise and anger on his face.

Mike immediately assumed the role of the tough guy. "Brother Partridge," he said contemptuously, why did you neglect to inform us that Compton had sent a shake-down letter to Harold Barnett?"

The indignant Partridge locked eyes with Mike. "It was an oversight. At the time I didn't make the connection between the letter and the murders." Jerry could see Partridge was fuming and not about to apologize. Mike had humiliated him before his council. Jerry knew that Mike was intentionally pushing him to see how he would react, because that little oversight made

Partridge a prime suspect as the Judas. Partridge stubbornly defended his position. "I know Compton is a fanatic and I can see why you might suspect him, but if my information is correct, you have no evidence to link him with the crime."

"If your information were correct, Brother Partridge," Mike retaliated, "you would know that Mr. Beal met privately with myself and Inspector Carmichael and gave us compelling information that makes Mr. Compton a prime suspect. Furthermore, Mr. Beal confided to us that he had good reason to believe the killers were tipped off Harold and Calvin would be together at 10:00 the morning of the shootings. He also said he suspected that someone on this council was the informant, because only the men on the council knew of the meeting. Our evidence supports Mr. Beal's theory. We believe that he learned the identify of the Judas and was killed before he could contact us."

Mike hesitated as his words sank in, scanning the room, looking at the apprehension and fear on the apostles' faces. The squelched Richard Partridge was the exception. His fleshy jowls trembled with anger. "Do you know who among us is the informant?" he thundered.

"Not at this point. It's just a matter of time and we will." Mike paused, looking each apostle in the eyes. A show of confidence. "But we need your help so we can bring this matter to a conclusion before someone else is murdered. That's why we're here. One of you killed Brigham Arthur Beal. We're not your enemy. We're trying to help you. You people are the victims here, not us, and only you have the information that will help us solve this case. By withholding information you are helping the killers."

Mike had not expected a sudden rush of information to come from the meeting. He knew the apostles would be afraid to volunteer information in front of their leader. Besides, they didn't know who among them they could trust.

"You can't blame them for not wanting to become a target," Jerry said. "A cut throat is a pretty grim way to die. But I predict that someone will come forward. I could see the gears spinning in their minds as you talked. It may take a little time, but someone will come forward."

"Yeah," agreed Mike. "Did you notice that Partridge was the only one who didn't seem to be afraid, and how he acted as if he had nothing to fear

"Not only that," Jerry added, "I liked the way he finally made a big show of cooperation as though he were an integral part of the investigation team. And the way he encouraged the council to come forward with any information that might be of help. It was his way of recovering from the chewing out you gave him."

"I know. At first I thought he might be our Judas, but he seemed legitimately upset about one of his apostles killing Beal. So far, he's still our best candidate, but his behavior today didn't support that theory. Unless he's one damned good actor."

Jerry thought, a *damned* good actor. "You know, Mike, both Partridge and Compton are exhibitionists. They like the limelight, it's all part of the illusion. Being a good actor is part of being a polygamist prophet."

Chapter Eight

THEIR FORD TURNED off the Ely Highway onto a graded dirt road that led west towards the foothills of Nevada's Ruby Mountains. High clouds streaked out of the northwest. Karris, who Mike had dubbed the two-eyed Cyclops, steered the car through the rocky dips and curves as fast as he dared. Dust billowed out from beneath the tires leaving a trailing cloud over the graveled road.

The hulking frame of Buck Jones was spread across the back seat, his head resting on the side window. Karris glanced at him through the rear view mirror, wondering how he could sleep. Each time they hit a bump, his shaggy head bounced off the glass.

They crested a hill, circled down through a ravine cut by a thousand flash floods, splashed through a creek bed of rippling water, and lugged their way up the other side. Karris maneuvered the Ford around a large outcropping of granite and dropped down into a thick grove of cedar and pinon trees. Far above them was a craggy peak splintered into steep canyons choked with aspen and pine.

On the other side of the grove, they suddenly burst upon a water tank, cluster of shanties and trailer houses surrounded by old cars, trucks, backhoes, and a rusty D-9 caterpillar. Below, on the alluvial plain, ugly gaping holes from placer excavations extended grotesquely for a half mile. Compton ordered, "Stop, this is the place."

It was nearly dusk. They sat there for a moment, looking down on the Coop mining camp. Children were playing keep-away with a ball. Two men stood by a jacked up car. No women were in sight. Smoke drifted from chimney pipes of ramshackle cabins, endowing the cool air with an aroma of pinion pine. Two dogs, one a German Shepard with bristling hair, barked an alarm.

Karris pulled alongside the largest of the clapboard dwellings. The beaten earth from foot traffic indicated that it was the main building. Compton walked in unannounced, followed by Jones and Karris. It was the communal kitchen and meeting room. He introduced himself to a woman wearing a long green dress and pink apron. Her gray hair was tied back in a bun. She asked, unsmiling, "Want something to eat?" It was the custom on the Nevada desert to greet visitors by offering food.

"I would, dear lady. And so would my companions."

They all took seats around a large wooden table still covered with crumbs from supper.

As the matronly woman hovered over the wood burning stove, she glanced at the three strangers making themselves at home as if they were invited guests. There was something ominous about the slender man with the goatee, the arrogant way he took charge, as if he had a right. And the two large, bearded men, their stony countenance and militant behavior was almost challenging. She sent a child for the man in charge. Sensing the precariousness of the situation, the boy ran down a dirt path to find Earl Baker, who was already en route to meet the intruders.

The coop people were noted for their feigned parsimony, and the conditions of the kitchen and the camp bore witness. The stove was fired by pinion and juniper that was plentiful in the mountains. The cupboards were clean, but made of pine and painted an ugly green. Knickknacks, doilies, and the other feminine artifacts that were routinely found in a kitchen to give spice to a woman's life, were conspicuously absent. Only the eating and washing necessities were present.

Jones and Karris were shoveling into their mouths the last morsels of venison stew when Earl Baker and four other men entered the kitchen. Compton didn't stand. He glanced up at them, then continued eating. Buck Jones tore off a chunk of homemade bread from a loaf and sopped up the gravy on his plate. Karris glared at Baker and the other men.

"What can we do for you men," Baker asked. He was a small man, no more than 5'7", dressed in overalls and a dirty ball cap that had "Hacienda" written in gold letters across the front. Compton replied arrogantly, "I'll be with you in a minute," and continued to eat.

It was rare that visitors came to the gold camp. Earl Baker, polite by nature, easily discerned that of the three intruders, the impertinent man was in charge. He couldn't help notice the size of the other two men. He wasn't afraid, but he didn't quite know how to handle the situation; he had never before been confronted with such arrogance. The man with the goatee was treating him as if he were the intruder; he knew he couldn't allow that. He whispered to the man next to him, "Tell Jake to get the shotgun and standby outside in case we need him." The man disappeared out the door.

"You men need to tell us who you are and what you want?"

Compton still ignored him. Jones and Karris sat patiently, watching. After Compton swallowed the last bite he looked up at Baker. "Why don't you sit down, friend?"

"We stay standing until we find out who you are and what you want."

Realizing that a confrontation was about to explode, Compton raised his right arm to the square, and said, "We come here in peace, brother, as emissaries of your Lord and Master, Jesus Christ. Now please sit down and I will tell you what brings us."

Baker and the others stared dumbfounded. The two were religious men, fundamentalists who embraced the Mormon faith, but they had not seen the likes of a missionary this brazen. Reluctantly, not wanting to aggravate a difficult encounter, they took seats across the table, remaining alert and tense. A pimply-faced youth with bushy eyebrows remained by the door.

"My name is Phillip Compton. The Lord Jesus Christ has personally called me to prepare the Saints for His swift coming during the millennium that is now upon us. He has sent me ahead as he did John the Baptist to call 'His House' to order. It is a wicked and evil generation that now controls His Church. They must repent and humble themselves before Him or they will not be able to abide His light." The words came swift and unencumbered. Baker and his men were aghast.

"The cleansing is to start among those who call themselves fundamentalists. If they obey the instructions that

I will impart, He will share with them new light and knowledge, and give to them the ordinances that will advance them to the celestial kingdom. Exaltation can be obtained in no other way. If those chosen to receive these oracles of peace and prosperity ignore them, they will be trodden under by the angels of death. Lo, the angels have already reaped their vengeance upon the wicked who refused to acknowledge the messages from His messenger. AND I AM THAT MESSENGER."

For five hours Compton preached in the dim light of a coal oil lamp, never tiring, ending as passionately as he had begun. Baker and the others sat erect and astonished, but unconvinced.

"The Lord has appointed me to collect his tithes. Those who cheat the Lord will be punished by the terrible fire of his tongue, and they will languish in hell until they have seen the error of their ways. He has already begun the execution and cleansing of those who refuse to obey. "

He did not mention Harold or Calvin Barnett by name, but by inference made it abundantly clear that their deaths were the direct result of insubordination to the law of tithing. Earl Baker was chilled by Compton's words for he had heard of the bloody murders of the Barnett brothers and the near decapitation of Brigham Arthur Beal. Word like that spread quickly from group to group. The mine had no telephone; nevertheless, Baker knew about the deaths the day following the murders. And now he knew that before him sat the grand reaper of their deaths.

Baker explained to Compton, "What you say is most interesting, but I don't have the authority to transfer funds of any kind. Dispersed money is made from the corporate office in Salt Lake City, and all disbursements must be approved by a committee of corporate officers."

Compton answered him with frigid contempt. "I will leave the matters of corporate red tape to you, but when I again return to the mine, I expect that proper arrangements will have been made for either me or my representative to pick up the first monthly tithe installment." A specific sum was not set. "The Lord God, your Master of the Universe, commands and demands His ten percent of the gross annual income in monthly payments. Your Creator and Advocate with The Most High is aware of the numerous thriving businesses controlled by His coop servants. He has blessed the people of the coop with prosperity and now he demands the interest of His investment." In Compton's diabolical mind that added up to hundreds of thousands of dollars each month.

Baker attempted to impress upon Compton that he should settle his demand for tithing with the central office, but Compton will not hear of it. He told the fidgety Baker, "As the anointed messenger of the Most High, I am holding you responsible for making good the tithing."

Beds were provided for Compton and his two henchmen.

While they slept, Baker sent a messenger to Salt Lake City with the news of Compton's visit.

After preaching most of the night, it was 10:00 A.M. before Compton, Jones, and Karris awakened. They went directly to the kitchen where they gorged themselves with scrambled eggs, hot tea, hamburger patties, and flapjacks prepared by the gray-haired lady. The weather outside had turned much colder and blustery. Karris opened the kitchen door and peered into the western sky; dark cumulus clouds filled the horizon. He said to the others, "We better get going, there's a storm coming."

The black clouds overtook them before they reached the Ely Highway. Swirling gusts of snow pelted the windshield. The wiper blades swung furiously back and forth. Karras rolled down the window, reached out with his left arm and tried to clear the ice from the blades. Cold air and snow blasted him in the face. Compton yelled, "Roll up the window. What's the matter with you?"

Within five minutes the ground, boulders, and sagebrush had turned powdery white. Snowflakes swirled in every direction. Unable to see, Karris slowed the car to a crawl. Finally forced to stop, he opened the door against the force of the wind. Once outside, fighting against the blinding snow and wind, he slammed the door and pulled the collar of his jacket tight around his thick neck. With bare hands, he clawed at the ice and snow on the windshield. Through squinting eyes he looked about him, it was a "white out."

He climbed back into the car, shivering, his bare head and shoulders covered with snow. "It's a 'white out', I can't see the road. We're going to have to wait it out."

The fury of the storm finally passed and the small driving pellets changed into a steady fall of wet flakes. At last the wipers were able to keep pace with the snow. But drifts had formed around the wheels. They had no shovel. With Compton behind the wheel spinning the tires, it took the combined strength of Jones and Karris to push the anchored car out of the drift.

In less than an hour, six inches of snow had fallen. The Nevada desert was totally white. With no tracks to follow, Karris was compelled to pick his way along the road grade, sighting between the snow-covered boulders and brush on either sides of the road. Twice he attempted to plow through two-foot snow drifts and got stuck. He and Jones were again forced to push. To make matters worse, the gas gauge was near empty. None of them had brought heavy coats and the car heater was the only way they could keep warm. It was another hour before the Ford approached the asphalt of the Ely Highway.

Just as they pulled onto the highway, an old four-wheel drive pickup truck from the north slowed and turned onto the snow-packed, gravel road. It was the two men Baker had sent to Salt Lake, returning with instructions.

The two Coop men had driven all night. They did not return with written instructions, the corporate decision was verbal: "Post sentries on the knoll overlooking the entrance to the mining camp. Compton and his men must be considered dangerous and responsible for the murders of the Barnett brothers. Arm yourselves and do what you feel is necessary to protect yourselves."

Jerry had tried unsuccessfully several times to establish a dialogue with the Coop group. Each contact had been cordial but unproductive. Therefore, he was surprised when he received a message to call Curt Goodson, one of the leaders of the group.

Goodson said he wanted to discuss Compton, but in person. Jerry would like to have met Goodson on Coop turf. It would have given him an opportunity to look around, but Goodson insisted on meeting Jerry at the District Attorney's Office. He arrived within minutes.

Curt Goodson was an unassuming man in his fifties, small in stature, dark hair and eyebrows. He was dressed like a farmer, light blue long-sleeved shirt, blue jeans, and work shoes. He was very ordinary in appearance and showed no signs of affluence in either his bearing or mannerisms. No one would have suspected that he controlled hundreds of thousands of dollars, possibly millions.

Goodson spoke slowly and deliberately, picking each word with care. "Phillip Compton and two of his men visited our Nevada mining camp. He wants us to pay him our tithing." He recounted to Jerry all the details as it had been given to him by the two messengers.

"Are you going to do it?"

"No! But we need to know where we stand with the law. We've posted guards on the road entering the camp. When he realizes we are not going to give him any money, we don't know what he'll do. From the way he talked to our man Baker, we believe it was him who killed Harold and Calvin Barnett."

"Did he say he had killed them?"

"Not in so many words. He said he was the Lord's messenger, and that the Lord had already started a cleansing by eliminating those who would not obey. To me, that's pretty clear he is behind the killings."

He handed Jerry some literature the Coop corporate office had received a month ago from Compton. The first page was a proclamation, written in the form of a revelation, allegedly from Jesus Christ, naming Compton as the vanguard of righteousness who had been called to prepare the way for the coming of Christ. The second page announced the new millennium and informed the Coop people that their tithes had been chosen to provide the funds to build the unpolluted temple from which Christ would reign through his servant, Phillip Compton.

Jerry set the papers on his desk and looked at Goodson. The color had gone out of Goodson's face. He waited patiently for Jerry's response.

"Well, there's no longer a question about a motive. You people are the real target. Killing the Barnett brothers was meant to be a sample of his power. I also suspect that with Harold Barnett out of the way, he has weakened the AJC making it more vulnerable to future plunder." He uttered a contemptuous chuckle. "He's no different than Al Capone. It's an elaborate shakedown making Jesus Christ a co-conspirator. The only difference between Compton and Capone is that Compton is using religion to extort dollars. Compton is selling protection and calling it tithing."

The isolation of the mining camp created a logistics dilemma for Goodson and Jerry. There were no telephones. They both envisioned Compton and his men riding into the camp, guns blazing. Goodson asked, "What if when they show up, we just blow them away."

The way Goodson asked the question, it was almost comical, so out of character. But Jerry could tell the mild mannered man was very serious. "You have the right to defend yourself, but you can't shoot them on sight just because they drive into camp." But Jerry was thinking that if they did blow them away, he couldn't blame them. "Tell your man Baker to report Compton's visit to the Ruby County Sheriff and I will call him myself so he knows the gravity of the situation. In the meantime I would furnish your men two-way radios or the best cell phones available. Sheriff Bud Stewart in Easterdale is doing his best to keep Compton under surveillance."

Jerry explained that the County Attorney stated they needed more evidence before they could pick up Compton. They needed to find the car and the shooters and connect them with Phillip Compton.

Jerry hoped that his meeting with Goodson would open the doors for future negotiations and expel the intrigue and mystery that surrounded the Coop group. He couldn't help but have respect for Goodson. Like many fundamentalists he was non threatening, ignoble in appearance and demeanor. As they talked, he volunteered a little information about his organization. He said their organization was economic-based and not religious, and only a few of their members embraced the Mormon faith. Jerry took that remark to mean that only a few practiced plural marriage. Nevertheless, he concluded that it was the work ethic, thrift, labor, and dedication to business that was the central theme and moving force of Coop success. It was unfortunate, Jerry contemplated, that some of the Coop people carried thrift to the extreme. Their obsession with obscurity, bordering abject poverty, only attracted unnecessary attention to themselves.

After telephoning the Ruby County Sheriff, Jerry contacted Mike and appraised him of the Goodson interview. They both agreed that there was no longer any question that Compton was their man. "Now all we have to do is prove it before he kills someone else," Mike said before he hung up.

The snow that blanketed the Nevada desert also hit Utah. It was the first major storm of the season and although it was a fierce storm, it melted rapidly except for the mountains above 6000 feet where it would remain until the following June.

Chapter Nine

IN THE INTEREST of time Mike and Jerry thought it best they interview the remaining witnesses one on one. After their meeting with Partridge and his council, it was important that Mike be available in the event one of the apostles decided he had information to share. It was also imperative that the leadership at Grass Valley be contacted to see if they had been harassed by Phillip Compton. In the meantime, Sheriff Bud Stewart and two of Mike's detectives were scouring the mountains and hills for the beige four-door sedan. One of Sheriff Stewart's reserve deputies owned a small Cessna 152 and was assisting in the search. It was a slow tedious job. One by one the dirt roads leading off the highway were followed until they terminated at a cabin, corral or just evaporated into the sage brush. Exploring these roads was more expedient from the air, but overall the search was handicapped by the six-inch blanket of snow. Cold air had moved in behind the storm slowing the melt. Furthermore, four-wheel drive pickups and snowmobiles were the only means of searching the canyons from the ground. After two fruitless days, the ground search was suspended unless something of interest was spotted from the air, then the Sheriff would dispatch pickups and snowmobiles to investigate further.

Parley P. Leatherbury was the first to contact Mike. They met at a coffee shop in the South Towne Mall. He was wearing a plaid waist-length coat and a Siberian fur hat. They took a booth in the corner. Leatherbury spoke first.

"I have been praying that the killers will soon be caught," he uttered softly.

"While you're at it pray for some warm weather," Mike answered impulsively.

Leatherbury gave him a quizzical look and said, "Alright."

Leatherbury was not tall, but he was big boned, barrel chested with broad shoulders, and his large head with thick, black hair was turning gray. He was powerfully built with a mismatched high pitched voice. He had the physique of a construction worker, but the temperament and charm of an office clerk. Mike suspected that his humble, condescending demeanor was a theatrical display.

Mike came directly to the point. "Do you have specific information?"

"Well, not really. My primary purpose is to establish a meaningful open line of communication and pledge my support to the capture of poor Harold, Calvin, Hilda, and Brigham's murderers."

Suspecting that Leatherbury had an ulterior motive in establishing a line of communication, Mike asked him the routine questions.

"No, I don't have a clue who the Judas might be. The apostleship is like a brotherhood. I love each and every man. It is beyond my imagination that one in the brotherhood would turn against the others."

Mike asked, "What about Phillip Compton? He was once a brother and now he's trying to shake you down."

"I know it looks bad for Phillip. I pray for him also. Phillip is suffering from delusions. The keys of the priesthood, I know, are here with our people." The sincerity in his voice dripped with honey. "I was well acquainted with Phillip when he was with us. We all were. I just hope and pray it was not

Phillip or someone else living the principle. We are a peace loving and humble people doing our best to live as God wants us. Over the years we have been persecuted like the Saints of old for our beliefs. We mean no harm to anyone. We stay to ourselves. We take care of our own problems. We do not force ourselves on anyone. Yes, we have our differences over who holds the keys, but as for me, I *know* where the keys are, but I do not hate my brothers because they disagree."

While Leatherbury was giving his little speech he looked deeply in Mike's eyes, his voice oscillating with emotion. His conviction and commitment seemed undeniable.

After bearing his soul to Mike, Leatherbury relaxed and grew more cordial and informal. Mike asked him, "Who among the apostles might be the Judas and who was vicious enough to bludgeon Brigham."

One by one, Leatherbury evaluated each apostle, describing his virtues. "I'm sorry," he said, "I can't find anything derogatory about any of my fellow apostles"

As Mike walked Leatherbury out to the parking lot, he thought, "This guy is so sweet and gentle he is incapable of seeing wickedness in anyone."

Before they parted, Leatherbury asked, "Has anyone besides me from the council contacted you?"

"I'm sorry, I can't answer that. Remember, I gave my word that any meeting would be kept strictly confidential."

"That's right, I forgot," Leatherbury said apologetically, "But I would like you to know that I am at your disposal night and day. If I can corroborate any new information , please call on me."

The air warmed and the snow melted on the lower elevations the further south Jerry drove. It was noon before he dropped down into Grass Valley.

Jerry wondered where they got the name Grass Valley because there was more red sand than there was grass. A few patches of snow on the north side of the houses remained. At the east end of the valley, red sandstone cliffs rose abruptly. At the base, on both sides of a narrow canyon, lay the clustered houses of the town.

The highway continued south. Jerry pulled off onto a smaller paved road that led towards the town a half mile east. As he approached, he passed an airstrip, a windsock fluttering in the breeze, and he noticed a new hanger large enough to house three small aircraft. A Leer jet parked to the side of the runway was lashed to the pavement. He estimated that Grass Valley town consisted of a hundred large dwellings, many in various stages of construction. He drove to the center of town and pulled into a service station and fast food store. Across the road was the church, a large box-like auditorium. Next to it was the school. It was recess time and children crowded the fenced playground. The kids swung, tossed balls, yelled, and ran. The boys were dressed like most country boys, except they all wore long-sleeved shirts. Without exception, all the girls were in ankle length, homespun dresses, their long hair in braids. They all seemed like regular kids.

Looking around he could see a mechanic's shop, post office, grocery store, and a pink stucco building with a red tile roof. A small wooden sign with black letters hung over the front door—Grass Valley City Hall. Parked in front was a police car with a single red bubble light on the roof.

Jerry was reminded that Grass Valley City was incorporated, with their own police department, water department, school district, fire department, and apparently their own airport. He also remembered reading that they had qualified for government grants used in the development of their water treatment plant and airport.

He decided to gas up before calling upon the local chief of police. Inside, the self-service station was patterned after most gas stops: the usual soda pop dispenser with cardboard cups, snacks, a cooler packed with bottled juices and more soda. A counter stretched across the back where a young lady fried hamburgers.

Jerry scrutinized the homely faces of the two female employees, while they in turn scrutinized him out of the corner of their eyes. They wore no makeup and their long hair was arranged on their heads so that a huge wave towered over their foreheads.

The women, like the men, were freckled with the country features typical of deep rural settlements. But there was something more than their lackluster and unfashionable appearance. And then it dawned on him; it was a lack of spirit or energy. There was a dullness in their eyes and they moved about mechanically. Somewhere between the playground and here, they got lost, Jerry thought.

Jerry thought it must happen when they marry. He guessed that from then on a married woman's day is the same, nothing to look forward to, no candlelight dinners, no theater, no anniversary bouquet of roses, no boxes of candy in fancy wrappings, no vacation on a sandy beach wading in the surf. Nothing to look forward to but the next baby.

The young lady behind the counter did not say hello, good afternoon, go to hell or anything. Even now as Jerry paid for the gas, her bland, unsmiling face offered no hint of her thoughts. Jerry gave her a friendly smile, but it had no effect. Yielding to an impulse he asked her, "Do you know where to find a turtle with no legs?"

Her lusterless eyes seemed to look past him and ever so timidly she replied, "No."

"Right where you left him," Jerry replied, this time flashing a mischievous grin.

The girl paused, thinking. Her cheeks turned rosy and her lips parted, stretching into a pretty smile. Her brown eyes lit up and she said, "Thank you," a dash of pep in her voice. As he started for the door, she called after him with unfeigned vitality, "Have a good day."

As he strolled to his car, the local cop jerked his car to a stop in front of him. It did not surprise Jerry. He had wondered how long it would take the men in charge to note his presence in town.

A middle-aged man wearing an Open Road Stetson and a star pinned to his cowboy shirt got out of the car, but left the motor running. He wore white canvas shoes and had a .357 Smith &Wesson strapped to his hip. He strolled up to Jerry who waited beside the front door of his car. The officer said, "Can I help you find somebody?"

"I've found him. It's you I'm looking for. I was just coming over to your office."

Jerry reached inside his coat producing his identification for the officer to examine. The officer bent over, squinting, looking first at the ID picture and then at Jerry.

Sounding as official as possible, Jerry said, "I am Inspector Gerald Carmichael of the Salt Lake District Attorney's Office."

The policeman's name was Dan Harlow. He informed Jerry that their ecclesiastic leader, Walt Banks, was down with angina pectoris and could not see anyone; however, his brother and mayor, Brad Harlow, was the one in charge.

The family resemblance between Dan and Brad Harlow, their doughy complexion, broad forehead, Roman nose, and thinning hair was unmistakable. In fact, later on, Jerry thought he detected Harlow genes in the facial features of everyone in Grass Valley. It was so noticeable that they could have passed for a separate race of people, and he wondered if it was from years of intermarriage.

The Harlow brothers immediately shifted into that friendly vernacular cop talk, as if they were regular law enforcement, but the Harlow boys were overusing it. Jerry guessed they picked it up attending crime conferences and police seminars.

They admitted that Phillip Compton had indeed been to

Grass Valley twice, the last time was a week before the Barnett murders. Compton had wanted to address the entire population of Grass Valley and expected the mayor to call a special town meeting. Phillip had been turned away both times

The first time Compton showed up, he was accompanied by two bearded men. The second trip, Compton came in force with four young men.

Dan Harlow said proudly, "We met force with force. I had five armed deputies backing me up. I told Compton we were a closed society and to take his literature and not come back."

Brad Harlow gave Jerry copies of the literature Compton had left. It was the same garbage he had mailed to Harold Barnett and left at the gold mine.

Dan Harlow, outspoken and blunt, predicted that Compton was behind the murders.

Brad Harlow volunteered, "I can remember the Compton family from the old days when I was a teenager. Everybody talked about how there was a streak of insanity in the family. Phillip had two brothers. One lived in a tepee in southern Utah waiting for God to arrive in a flying saucer. The other brother tried to cut his mother's throat and was committed to the Utah State Hospital. Like Phillip, he thought he was the One Mighty and Strong and went crazy when his mother tried to convince him otherwise." Jerry concluded his visit, eager to return to Salt Lake and see what Mike had turned up.

Lazarus Quintana was the next apostle to meet with Mike. Lazarus had come to Salt Lake for the funerals. He was the apostle over the Elk Creek Ranch in the rolling sagebrush hills of northwestern Utah. Quintana was a rugged, authentic cowboy, with a weather-beaten face and strong callused hands. He had been told by another apostle that an informant was hiding among the apostleship. Because he was busy raising sheep and cattle, he was not privy to the inter-group politics and had no idea who the informant might be. But he was visibly upset with what Partridge was doing.

Partridge had divided all the assets of the AJC into nonprofit corporations. The Elk Creek Ranch was now a nonprofit charitable organization owned by Richard Partridge, Parley P. Leatherbury, and Marvin Heywood. Quintana was upset because it had been him that developed the ranch and made it a profitable undertaking, and he was not named on the corporate papers. He knew that without him and his sons the ranch would fall to pieces, so he planned to use that ploy to get his name added to the corporation.

The same three men, he said, had formed another corporation called Communities of the Apostolic Order. The CAO had been recorded with the State of Utah as a nonprofit religious organization and theoretically was supposed to be patterned after the united order. About a hundred families had built on what was once priesthood-owned property, but now belonged to the CAO. Partridge and his lawyers drew up an "occupation agreement," a contract of sorts and were coercing all the members to sign it. Partridge, as the Presiding Elder of the corporation, had absolute power. The occupation agreement allowed Partridge to evict without enumeration anyone he decided was out of harmony with the Apostolic Order. Lazarus Quintana was livid and had called Partridge's actions communistic, criminal, and priestcraft. But he was afraid to confront Partridge for fear he would be driven off the Elk Creek Ranch, the only home he had ever known. Mike advised him to contact an attorney, but was afraid that there was nothing that could be done unless Partridge was abusing the nonprofit status.

Brian Johnson met with Mike in the parking lot of the Fashion Place Mall. They sat in Mike's unmarked Ford. Johnson was nervous and slumped down in the seat, alert for danger. At first Mike thought he was pretending fright, but when a black car drove within a few feet of them and Johnson hunkered down beneath the dashboard, he knew the fright was for real.

The man made Mike promise their conversation would be confidential and he would not be called to testify—under any circumstance. He was very much like Brigham Arthur Beal, small in stature, meek in appearance and personality.

After he had calmed down, he said, "Me and Brigham were very close. He was the only one I knew besides Harold that could keep a secret. The morning before Brigham was killed, he stopped by my house in Midvalley. We talked for about fifteen minutes." He looked all around before continuing. "Brigham was very secretive. He told me he had narrowed down the informant to three people, Richard Partridge, Parley P. Leatherbury, and Marvin Heywood. Brigham said that by the end of the day he expected to know which of the three was the Judas."

Brain Johnson once again swivelled his head back and forth, watching the approaching cars. "My life is not worth a nickel if they find out I'm talking to you."

"Who are 'they'?"

He replied, "Whoever killed Brigham and Harold."

Mike tried to assure him that they would provide all the protection he required if he could give them concrete proof of the Judas. He even offered to put him in a hotel, but the man declined.

Mike asked, "Why did Brigham suspect these three?"

"To begin with," he said, "all three were friends of Phillip before he left, particularly Richard. Richard and Phillip were always trying to change the status quo and often teamed up together, trying to influence Harold. Richard Partridge has always wanted to take the tithing and invest it in money-making ventures. Harold wouldn't let him. Now Richard is the leader and displays no remorse over Harold's death. He has inferred that God removed Harold because he was a weak leader."

"What can you tell me about Leatherbury?" Mike asked.

"He pretends to be a dedicated follower but is really very ambitious and wherever the money flows, there is Parley P. Leatherbury. He is the most militant of the apostles and likes to use the Danites as an example of uncompromising loyalty. On several occasions he has asked new converts if they are willing to do whatever is necessary to protect the life of the prophet and defend the priesthood, even if it means taking the life of an enemy. He and Partridge seem to be of one mind, but it is a closeness that is built upon fear, as if Leatherbury is holding something over Richard's head."

"What about Heywood?"

"Marvin Heywood is a 'yes' man and aligns himself with whoever is the strongest," Johnson said with disgust. "He can't make it on his own. Phillip Compton was always picking his brain. Richard Partridge still does, and so does Parley Leatherbury. But I think Marvin would defect to the Grass Valley people if they would make him an apostle. He likes the way they control the women. Like Parley, he pretended to be loyal to Harold."

"Do you think the Judas intends to turn the AJC over to Compton?"

"Not unless it's Heywood. The AJC is too lucrative to turn over to someone else. It's my guess that whoever the Judas is, he used Compton to get rid of Harold and Calvin to make room for himself."

"If you're right, that would tend to eliminate Heywood as a suspect."

"Yes, but he could still be the Judas. He's not strong enough to gain the backing of the apostles, but if he helped hand the AJC over to Compton, it would make him a big man and the AJC would go back to being a closed society."

Mike thought for a minute. "From my point of view, Partridge and Leatherbury are the strongest and most greedy among the apostles. They wouldn't abdicate to Compton. If

Heywood is our man, then Partridge and Leatherbury could be next on the hit list."

Chapter Ten

THE PILOT OF the Cessna 152 noticed the snow melting and sliding off the tin roofs of cabins in the mountains. The warming trend meant another storm might be on its way, so Sheriff Stewart called the Highway Patrol and asked if they would use their aircraft to assist in the search.

Three planes crossed the mountains for five hours, landing and refueling and taking off again. It was the Sheriff's pilot in the Cessna 152 that finally hit pay dirt two hours before dark. Peeking out from under snow-flocked branches in a gully near an abandoned mine was the hood of a late model, beige-colored car. The pilot said it looked like the vehicle had been pushed off the road down the rocky incline into the juniper trees. When Mike heard the good news he let out a war whoop and called Jerry on his cell phone. Jerry, Beth, and Katherine were just sitting down in a booth at the Balsam Hideaway.

Katherine had arrived first. This was her first meeting with Beth. A waiter asked if she would like a drink and she declined. As she waited, she began having second thoughts about meeting Jerry's wife. She wondered if she was overdressed and if her hair was still in place; she impulsively patted the blond hair on the back of her head.

Jerry and Beth arrived moments later. The women dined on Atlantic Salmon and Jerry ordered prime rib, end cut. Beth and Katherine did most of the talking.

Katherine presented her case beginning with the dissertations of Brigham Young. Beth tried to counter with the dictum that modern prophets superseded the dead prophets. The women were extremely courteous and treated each other's argument with the greatest respect. Katherine allowed Beth to take the offensive while she defended her position. Jerry devoured the prime rib while he listened with fascination. He admitted to himself that his experiences with polygamists, especially the honest ones trying to live a good life, were causing him to rethink the overall issue.

On the way home, Beth agreed that Katherine was far too pretty and sophisticated to waste her life as a polygamist. Until now, she had assumed that women who entered polygamy were homely and would have difficulty finding a monogamous husband. Beth vowed not to give up until she had rescued Katherine.

Mike and Jerry left before daylight, followed by the Sheriff's Mobile ID wagon. After they arrived at Easterdale, it was another forty-five minutes to the dirt road that lead to the deserted mining camp where the beige vehicle was spotted. The Sheriff did not think a wrecker could make it to the mining camp until more snow melted. Three four-wheel-drive vehicles and four snowmobiles, if needed, were waiting to transport them the five miles into the hills. The two ID specialists gathered into a valise, finger print brushes, colored dust, plastic bags, and camera.

It took another forty-five minutes to plow their way to the sight. The snowmobiles in the back of two pickup trucks were not needed.

Everybody was dressed in heavy boots, wool shirts, and quilted jackets. The vehicle, a late model four-door Pontiac, was wedged against a large pinion tree about thirty feet down a gully. Climbing down, the footing was rocky and slick. The automobile was in good shape for having bounced through the rocks. The only observable damage was a popped trunk lid and two flat front tires. Of course they couldn't see the undercarriage.

Before touching the vehicle, it was photographed from every angle beginning with where it was pushed off the road. There could be no doubt that whoever disposed of the vehicle did not want it found.

The Crime Lab boys had first access. For a half hour they dusted for fingerprints without lifting a single print, inside or out; it had been wiped clean. A portable vacuum was used to sweep the back seat and floor, the contents placed in plastic bags. Wool fibers were found that may have come from the suspect's sweater. They swept and vacuumed the front seat and floor. Nothing of significance was found. When ID was done, Mike and Jerry checked the glove compartment, it was empty—no registration. Jerry noticed the license plates had been removed and said to Mike, "They didn't want to make it easy on us, did they?"

Mike replied, "I'll get the motor number. I'll bet they didn't think of erasing it."

Under the front seat, lodged against a bracket, Mike found a single, empty .22 cartridge. It was placed in a plastic bag. The firing pin mark would be compared with the firing pin mark of the empty shell recovered at the murder scene.

The trunk contained the usual things: spare tire, jack, lug wrench, two greasy mechanic's rags, and a crumpled tan sweater with dark brown reindeer heads across the chest. Mike let out a war whoop. They theorized the sweater was used to wipe down the vehicle.

The batteries on Mike's cell phone had just enough strength to call the dispatcher to run the motor number on the DMV computer. The vehicle was registered to a Nancy Cooper at a Salt Lake City address. Nancy had reported it stolen to the Salt Lake City Police at 4:00 P.M the day Harold and Calvin were murdered.

When they got back to Easterdale, Jerry called Richard Partridge from the Sheriff's Office. Partridge said Nancy was married to Douglas Cooper, a former member of AJC who had defected with Phillip Compton. Partridge thought that Douglas and Nancy had separated. He said Douglas was a young man in his late twenties, about 5'10", light brown hair, blue eyes, not set close together. Jerry asked him to prepare a list of every male who followed Compton together with his description and where he lived.

Wanting a second confirmation, Mike called Brian Johnson and asked him about Douglas Cooper. Brian repeated what Partridge had said, but added, "I heard Douglas was interested in Marvin Heywood's daughter, Rachel. I can't understand why Marvin would allow an apostate to date his daughter, but then it's none of my business."

Johnson also informed Mike that Douglas Cooper was a self employed building contractor and that he was a mild mannered individual thoroughly mesmerized by Compton. Mike asked Johnson to also prepare a list of the Compton defectors, with physical descriptions. Johnson did not know of anyone with narrow eyes.

A discussion was held between Sheriff Stewart, Jerry, Mike, and two of Mike's detectives. The next logical step was to confront Compton and ask to interview Cooper. But the chances of Compton cooperating would be nil. If and when contact was made, it was agreed Sheriff Stewart should be the spokesman because Compton had not yet severed communication with him. In the meantime, it was decided a telescopic camera surveillance should be set up in a nearby house. Mike volunteered his two detectives.

It was late when Mike and Jerry arrived back in Salt Lake. They went directly to the home of Nancy Cooper. She lived in the old section of Kearns, a low income housing project built toward the end of World War II. Lights were still on so they knocked on the door.

Nancy was brown haired, thin with sallow cheeks, and had the look of anorexia. Mike thought that with a little flesh on her bones she could be a pretty women. She wore a long plain dress flowered in shades of pink with a white collar. She portrayed the typical fundamentalist.

Nancy was pleasant and cooperative. She took them into the kitchen where they sat at the table while three toddlers watched television in the front room.

Mike attempted to be as gentle as he could. "We found your Pontiac in the mountains southwest of Easterdale. Someone pushed it in a gully. If it doesn't snow again, a wrecker should be able to pull it out in the next few days."

"I have insurance if that will help."

"Call your insurance agent and he will tell you what to do from there." They didn't tell her that they suspected her husband was involved in the murders. "We think whoever pushed your car into the ravine was from Easterdale. If you could help us locate Douglas, he might have information that will help."

Nancy said, "The last time I saw Douglas was the day my car was stolen. Two weeks ago, Douglas traded his blue 1998 Dodge pickup for my car. He said he had priesthood work to do and it would be better if he were in a car. The afternoon he brought it back it was stolen, right in front of the house, while he was inside visiting with me and the kids. Can you imagine. Douglas left the keys in the ignition."

Nancy offered to fix them a cup of herbal tea and started to clear a place at the table, but they both declined. "Douglas and I separated when he joined Phillip Compton." She looked at Mike, then Jerry, to see how they would react. Their expressions were nonjudgmental. "I did not trust Phillip," she continued. "I refused to move to Easterdale. We are still friendly though. Lately Douglas has been attempting to patch up our differences, hoping to get back together for the children's sake. He wants a plural wife." She again looked at the detectives to see how they reacted to plural wife. Nothing. "He wants a plural wife so bad he was willing to do almost anything. You see, not having a plural wife in a polygamous group is like polygamous women not able to have children. Raising up a righteous seed is what it's all about."

Jerry asked, "Did Douglas abuse you?"

"Heavens no. He's not the aggressive type. He's so timid he has difficulty relating to women. That's part of why he can't find a plural wife. Lately, he has been courting Marvin Heywood's daughter, Rachel."

Glancing again at the detectives, she said, "In polygamy a married man can court another single women. Douglas asked me how I felt about Rachel. I told him he ought to take care of his first family before he started looking for a plural wife.

"Our problems began when Philip started leading Douglas around on a leash. If he strayed too far, he was yanked back. Compton is forever finding important priesthood things that need Douglas' attention. Douglas couldn't see that he was neglecting his business and his children. I tried to reason with him, I tried everything I could think of to get him away from Compton. But Douglas thought Compton was a God and he had to please him. Do you know what Douglas told me? 'Priesthood work comes before family. Without priesthood, there is no family.' I told Douglas, 'you got it all wrong. The priesthood is supposed to serve the family, not the family serve the priesthood.' "

Jerry sympathized as she forced each word. Her hazel eyes were sunk in with dark blotchy bags beneath. Still in her early twenties, she looked used up from giving birth to babies too close together. Jerry suspected her lethargy was mental as well as physical. There was a hopelessness about her as if fate had dealt her a low blow and she was powerless to stop it. He asked, "Do you need food or medicine?"

"No, thank you, I'm fine," and forced an embarrassed smile. "I have sufficient for my needs. I'm on food stamps and I make a little money cleaning homes with my sister."

Mike asked, "Do you know where Douglas is staying?

"I don't. Since he moved out and joined Phillip, he doesn't tell me a thing. He won't even mention the names of his friends. I''m sorry I'm no help."

"What about a man with narrow set eyes?" Jerry asked.

"Nope," she replied, the fatigue in her voice and strain on her face told them they better leave.

After climbing into the car, Mike leaned back, smiling. "And she said she was sorry she couldn't be of more help. Next stop, Rachel Heywood."

Chapter Eleven

THE UNCERTAIN FUTURE of Katherine dominated Beth's mind. Katherine was not at all like Beth expected, like the polygamists she had seen in grocery stores, drab in appearance, no makeup, long hair done up in waves and swirls cemented together with a sticky gel. Katherine was everything they were not—vibrant, well dressed, naturally beautiful, not to mention her regal bearing. Impulsively, she called Katherine and they lunched on salad, shrimp, and crab. They discussed children, the decadent affects of TV, and the hullabaloo over Y2K. Suddenly, Katherine turned gloomy and poked at bits of crab with a fork. Beth waited, knowing that something was on her mind. It only took a few seconds and Katherine poured out her feelings about Richard Partridge.

She confided that Partridge had summoned her to his office, closing the door so that they were alone. He sat her down and, while standing over her, revealed that he had been visited by an angel with a sword poised to strike. In a clear powerful voice, the angel declared that it had been foreordained that he marry Katherine Sinclair and warned him that if he did not, his head would be lopped off.

Katherine said she was stunned. What could she say to him? His proposal was totally unexpected. This was the *prophet* talking, *the man who held the keys.*

She said to Beth, "Richard has a repulsive habit of coughing up phlegm and either spitting or swallowing it. I don't think he realizes how disgusting that is. And he coughs and swallows right after telling me I'm supposed to marry him."

With pursed lips and wrinkled nose she told how he bent over to kiss her and when she smelled his bad breath, she instinctively turned away. He hesitated as if unsure how to proceed, so he tenderly kissed her on the neck. It made her skin crawl.

"I guess I should be flattered," she said sourly, "that the Lord has chosen me to be the wife of his prophet. But, Harold, before he died, told me not to trust in the arm of flesh and to obtain a witness of my own that a principle is correct. I do not have a spiritual witness that I am to marry Richard Partridge, nor do I want one."

Beth could not hide her revulsion. "Katherine, you cannot possibly believe an angel would do that? The man's lying. It was his way of cutting you out for himself."

The two women discussed the dilemma. If Katherine refused to marry Richard Partridge, it would be tantamount to denying that he's a prophet. And Beth was pleased. What better predicament to prove to Katherine the fraud and deception of polygamist prophets. Katherine agreed with Beth that a true prophet of God would not behave in that manner.

Beth munched on her salad, lost in thought as Katherine continued to talk.

Later that afternoon Beth's telephone rang. "Wait until I tell you the latest," Katherine said, and related what had happened.

Parley P. Leatherbury had just paid her a visit. In the privacy of the parlor, he impressed upon Katherine the ominous impact of his three recurring dreams. Apparently, Parley considered three the magic number that gave his dreams credibility. Each dream, he said, was identical, and in each dream he and Katherine were wed. He said he did not accept them as prophecy until the third dream, at which time he was filled with the spirit. He said that when he finally acquiesced, the angels in heaven rejoiced. He predicted that as his wife, she would reign supreme as a queen and be the most powerful woman in the group.

Katherine said that she very calmly sat the excited Parley down and told him about Richard's angel and sword. Parley was speechless and had the look of a child caught with his hand in the cookie jar, his jowly cheeks quivering. Katherine asked sweetly, "Do you suppose the Lord wants me to marry both of you?"

Color returned to his face and wheels began spinning in his head. His pious composure returned and he looked at Katherine with the dignity of a patriarch and prophet, "That's exactly what the Lord wants."

Katherine moaned. "Beth, it's not the answer I expected. I thought I was being smart and had trapped him in his deceit. Now I'm in deeper than ever."

"So I asked him, are you suggesting that I be polyandrous? And he told me yes, that in special cases it was permitted. Beth, I nearly fainted."

"But whose wife will I be in the Celestial Kingdom?" she asked him. He told her she would belong to both of them. Her lot would be polyandrous in the next life as well. He tried to make it sound as if she would be a queenly woman of high rank. But she did not see the situation at all matriarchal, but rather a woman passed from one man to another.

"If I have a baby, how will I know who is the father?"

He didn't see where that would be a problem inasmuch as

it was an honor for a child to be the son or daughter of either himself or Richard. No matter what obstacle she threw in his path, he found a way around it. She soon grew weary and excused herself, begging Parley's pardon. She told him she had to think and he said he understood. Before departing he reminded her, "The Lord has selected you for a special purpose, as important as the mission of Mary, mother of Jesus Christ."

Beth hissed with disgust. "We have got to get you out of there before every man in the group comes sniffing around with some screwball revelation." Beth volunteered to assist Katherine in finding an apartment or duplex, but Katherine said she had already found one, on the other side of the valley. She would make the move that night, taking only what was needed. The bulk of her belongings were in storage and the location a secret.

As disgusting as the experience was for Katherine, Beth was glad it happened, for now she knew that Katherine was on her way out of polygamy.

Mike pounded on the front door while Jerry surveyed the junk and old cars littered about the yard. The door opened and five half-naked kids, all diaper age, food smeared across their awestruck faces, stood staring up at them.

"Hello," Mike said, smiling. "Is your daddy home?" A little boy broke away from the group and darted toward the stairs. Cold air poured into the open doorway. Mike asked if they could come inside out of the cold just as a teenaged girl in tight jeans and sweatshirt came out of the kitchen. She pushed the children aside and invited them in. Jerry asked the young lady her name, and she said, "Rachel."

Jerry studied her. She was clean, well developed, and he guessed about eighteen years old. Had he seen her on the street he would not have guessed she came from a polygamous family. As she spoke, she seemed reasonably intelligent and self assured, with a flattering, coquettish charm that immediately captured one's attention. Cosmetics accentuated her brown eyes and the bluish eye shadow gave her an exotic, Egyptian glow. He was trying to decide if her seductive posture was genetic, or deliberate, when Marvin came down the stairs holding his head slightly to one side as if he had the weight of the world on his shoulders.

He held in his hand a Book of Mormon, giving the appearance of one who had been assiduously studying, so much so that he hadn't shaved for three days. As he drew near, perceiving that the two men were strangers, the weighty look of preoccupation changed to one of worry. After Mike and Jerry displayed their identification and shook his clammy hand, his countenance slipped from worry to unrestrained anxiety and the two detectives knew that Marvin Heywood would tell them anything they wanted to know.

They sat on the tattered old couch, sinking deep into the cushions. Rachel swept aside a pile of laundry to make room. Marvin pulled up a straight-backed chair and sat down in front of them. Rachel started for the kitchen when Mike called out, "Rachel, we would like you to stay. We want to talk to you also." The blood drained out of Marvin's face. Children gawked from the doorways until Ramona, one of Marvin's plural wives, swept them away like a mother hen with her chicks.

Mike and Jerry sat calmly, silently, waiting while the anxiety inside Marvin curdled and ripened. Rachel, unaware of the stress boiling inside her father, stood behind him, her weight resting appealingly on one leg, chest pushed out, her pretty face smirking, obviously enjoying this sudden thrush of attention.

Before the silence became unbearable, Jerry spoke. Looking into Marvin's brown eyes he said sympathetically, "Would you like to tell us about it?"

"About what?" A slight quiver, almost a stutter in his

voice, fear mounting. Both detectives wondered, have we found our Judas?

"You know, what's bothering you."

"Do I need a lawyer? I can't afford one."

"Any time you are questioned by a policeman you are entitled to have an attorney present and if you can't afford one, the court will appoint one." Jerry spoke as if they were friends and that he understood Marvin's dilemma, and already knew what he was about to reveal. "It depends on how much you tell us or how much you don't tell us. And of course you realize that whatever you say can be used against you in a court of law. You just go ahead and tell us about it, we'll understand, and it will go to your credit that you cooperated."

Marvin struggled to control his fear and clear his mind. Should he wait and confide in an attorney? But then the detectives seemed to already know. If they did know, they were not outraged. Marvin had dreaded this day, down deep knowing that it would come. Now that it was here he wanted to get it over as quickly and as painlessly as possible. If he refused to talk and waited for an attorney, he would undoubtedly be arrested and thrown in jail. Then the newspapers would find out, all the people in the group would find out. Sensing Jerry's compassion, his anxious expression metamorphosed into desperation and hope. Marvin asked, "Can we work it out, just us three?"

"First, tell us about it. Let's see if we have our facts right," Jerry gently urged.

"I don't know where to start. At first all I wanted to do is see how she was developing. I thought it was a father's prerogative. And then I felt I should teach her what to expect about sex. I know I shouldn't have touched her, but I swear to God, Rachel and I have not had sex."

Mike and Jerry looked up at Rachel; her face was flushed. Not knowing what to say, her forehead furrowed and she gave a shrug. They then glanced at each other, holding back their surprise.

Mike said, "Tell us about Douglas Cooper."

"I just wanted to make some money, is all." And then Marvin broke down and told them the whole sordid story, how he was using Rachel to seduce young suitors and charging them a dowry.

Mike, playing the tough guy, got in Marvin's face and in a threatening manner, asked him point-blank, "Did you tip Compton off about Harold and Calvin?" Marvin swore up and down he was not the Judas. Near tears, he pleaded, "You have got to believe me."

"What about Brigham Arthur Beal, did you cut his throat?" By that time both Mike and Jerry knew he was not their man. Marvin was a pathetic pervert, a pedophile preying on his own children, using his priesthood authority to justify his debauchery. The sudden exposure had brought him back to reality and reduced him to a pitiful creature in a human body. His guilt was so great that he curled up fetal-like in his chair.

When they were through with Marvin they pulled up a chair for Rachel. She too held nothing back. They explained that they could not allow her and her father to be in the same house, there was also the other children to think about. For the time being, they would have to arrest him which would take him out of the house. They reassured her he would get help for his sickness, but she didn't seem to care one way or the other.

And then they asked her when Douglas was expected back. She said, "Tonight at 7:00."

Jerry called Beth to inform her he'd be working late. They just got a big break in the Barnett murders. She asked what it was and he said he would tell her later.

"Okay, dear," she replied, "maybe I'll invite Katherine over, I'm making great progress."

"You two are getting pretty thick," he teased.

"Don't worry, it's for a good cause," then he hung up.

Marvin's wives and children appeared to take the arrest of Marvin in stride. Plain clothes detectives from the Juvenile Division were summoned and took him to jail. Arrangements were then made for the women and children to spend the night with friends, except for Rachel. Mike informed the Captain and dispatcher they would be on a stakeout. Two additional detectives were assigned to stand by in the neighborhood ready to move in if there was trouble. Mike and Jerry took positions in the kitchen. At exactly 7:00, they heard a knock at the front door.

"The poor bastard really has the hots for little sexy Rachel," Mike whispered. Jerry smiled back agreement.

They could hear the muffled voices of Rachel and Douglas. Giving Douglas a chance to settle himself, Rachel excused herself and came into the kitchen. "Okay, he's on the couch."

Jerry and Mike entered the living room, Mike's hand on the holstered Smith & Wesson, semiautomatic. Rachel said to Douglas, "These men want to talk to you," and then she quickly retreated to the kitchen. Douglas was at a distinct disadvantage seated deep in the couch. Jerry flashed his badge and ID with his left hand, leaving his right hand free. "We are police officers, keep your hands on your knees where we can see them."

Douglas did not try to stand or protest. He remained seated, dumbfounded, doing as instructed.

Mike had his semi-automatic out. "Sorry to spoil your evening, Douglas, but you are under arrest. Please stand and turn around with your hands outstretched."

While Jerry handcuffed Douglas behind his back and patted him down, Douglas asked timidly, "What am I under arrest for?"

"For littering," Mike replied.

"Littering?" Surprise in his voice.

"That's right. For pushing your wife's Pontiac into a gully." Mike paused before thundering the next remark. "And the murder of Harold, Calvin, and Hilda Barnett—not to mention poor little Brigham Arthur Beal."

Instinctively, Douglas blurted out, "I had nothing to do with Beal," and then caught himself.

He was visibly shaken, standing on wobbly knees, incapable of resistance. Mike's actions conveyed to Douglas that it was a "done deal" as they advised him of his rights. Jerry behaved as if the arrest was routine and just part of the job. They knew of course it was the worst day of Douglas' life. His reaction was the same as Marvin's. His mind was cluttered with fear, guilt, and self destruction. He was alone, far away from the charismatic strength of Phillip Compton. The great cause and the bloodletting of the Barnetts now seemed hollow and devoid of virtue. There was no buoyant background music or angels singing support. There was nothing to give him comfort or encouragement, only the stark reality that he had assisted in the senseless murder of three people for a man he had loved more than his wife.

They took him to Mike's office on the 10th floor of the Hall of Justice in downtown Salt Lake City. The handcuffs were removed.

Douglas was not a big man. Although lean and fit from years of carpenter labors, his demeanor was mild and respectful. If he were to bolt and try to escape, they were confident they could restrain him. Besides, there were five other detectives just outside Mike's office awaiting the results of the interrogation.

Douglas, resigned to his fate, asked, "What happens from here?"

"We are going to have to book you. But before we do, you said you didn't have anything to do with killing Beal. We need to get that resolved. But first, let us advise you of your rights once again."

He did not need to ponder. His overwhelming guilt would not permit him do anything but confess. What he desired most at that moment was to be punished, to be flogged, to offer himself up as a sacrifice and atonement. Phillip had promised that the Lord would protect them. He had given each one of them a reassuring priesthood blessing. Douglas was confused and flooded with doubt.

Once Douglas started talking he found it hard to stop because the more he revealed, the better he felt. It was like ridding himself of a terrible burden. He said Phillip told them the keys had been taken away from Harold because he was a lethargic prophet who would not take up the sword in building up the kingdom. He needed to be eliminated so that God's work could carry on.

Douglas sat in a corner chair while Mike occupied the seat behind the desk and Jerry sat in the chair next to the closed door. Outside the window the city lights lit up a starless sky.

He convinced the detectives that no one in Phillip's group had killed Brigham. It might have been Phillip's confederate in the Barnett group. He didn't know who the confederate was.

Douglas give up the names of the three young shooters. "When we left Phillip," he said, "we were like zombies. It was not until the end of the day before the full wallop of what we had done hit us. And then we were scared to death."

Douglas said he watched from the corner of his eyes the lady who pulled into the parking lot, doing his best not to be conspicuous. Because the motor was running, she kept glancing at him suspiciously. He said he thought Edger Dressler, the man in charge, was going to kill her. He didn't want that, she was innocent. He said he thought Dressler would have run up behind and shot her in the head if they hadn't begged him to get in the car so they could get out of

there. Douglas said for a minute or two Dressler wasn't
listening. It was not until the guys in the back seat also
shouted at him to get in the car that his mind changed. The
shouting, which the woman never heard, saved her life.

Mike asked him if Dressler had narrow set eyes. He
thought for a minute, and shook his head no. He turned to
Jerry and shrugged.

Douglas said when they got safely back to Easterdale,
Dressler said he should have followed his instincts and shot
the women. Of the four, Dressler was the least repentant. He
took morbid delight in describing to Phillip how surprised
Harold had been when they burst in from the kitchen, and how
foolish and powerless Harold appeared crumpled and bloody
on the floor. He made it sound to Phillip like he was as cool
and collected as a Mossad assassin.

Douglas said it was the lady in the parking lot that prompted
them to dump the car. Phillip tried to comfort them by saying,
"God will cloud that woman's mind and she will remember
nothing. But to play it safe he said to get rid of the car."

The names of the two other men were Herb Lowder, age
seventeen, and Carl Beckstead, nineteen. Dressler was
twenty-seven. Herb wore the sweater. All three, Douglas
said, were hid out in the stone church where they had enough
guns and ammunition to hold off an army.

He said it was stupid of him to visit Rachel, but he
couldn't help himself. He confided that he was in love with
Rachel and he knew she was in love with him. And then he
fell silent, looking out the window at the city lights. Remorse
swelled and he began having second thoughts. What if Phillip
really was a prophet. Had he let Phillip and God down? Did
this mean he would never be with Rachel? He couldn't get her
out of his mind. Her grasp on him was intoxicating. He had
wanted to serve God with all his might, mind and strength,
and now he had made a mess of everything. What had seemed
so right, so predictable, was now wrong. He had told

everything, there was nothing left. Had he done right? With nothing left to say his mind returned to the precariousness of his predicament. It was not so much the punishment that upset him as what people would think. He did not know if he could face that.

He asked Mike for another drink of water. Mike left the office. He returned after a minute and asked Jerry to step outside the office, closing the door behind him so Douglas couldn't hear. "I called the County Attorney. He said we will have to wait until in the morning before we can obtain warrants. No judge available. He suggested we isolate Douglas in a separate cell." Jerry agreed that was a good idea.

When Jerry went back into Mike's office, Douglas Cooper wasn't sitting in his chair. The large window was open, the curtains swayed in the cold breeze. Jerry's heart dropped to his stomach. "Mike," he called out, rushed to the window and looked down expecting to see Douglas splattered on the cement below. He wasn't there.

"I'm right here." It was Douglas, sitting on the eighteen-inch ledge to Jerry's left, just out of arms length, his feet dangled over the side.

"What the hell you doing out there?" Jerry tried to remain calm.

Mike peeked over Jerry's shoulder. "Oh crap," he said, "we're in trouble now."

Douglas gazed at Jerry through blurry eyes. "I've made a mess of things," he said.

"Come back in," Jerry appealed, "we can work this out."

Mike yelled out the window, "Cooper, get your ass back in here." The command didn't phase Douglas who just sat there drearily, gazing out at the city lights. At that point, Mike was more frightened than Douglas, "What the hell am I going to tell the Sheriff if he jumps," he whispered to Jerry. "Cooper," he yelled again, "get your ass back in here before I come out after you."

Douglas looked over at Jerry, "If he comes out here I"m going to jump."

By that time the rest of the detectives had stormed into the office, worried looks on their faces. One of them said, "I didn't even know you could open the damned windows."

Jerry ushered them all out of the office except for Mike. "Let me talk to him, Mike, we've got to be easy with him or he will jump."

"What the hell we going to do. The little bastard. Maybe if we got Rachel up here?"

"Good idea," Jerry replied. "Have someone go get her in case we need her."

Jerry poked his head out the window. Douglas was holding his head in his hands, sobbing, unconcerned with the height. Jerry said ever so cautiously, "Douglas, let's talk about it."

Douglas glanced over at him, tears streaming down his cheeks. "What's to talk about. I've made a mess of things."

"You can't blame yourself," he replied, "Douglas, it's kind of awkward sticking my head out and twisting around, would you mind if I just sat here in the window while we talked?"

"Not as long as you stay there," he replied.

Jerry climbed up onto the window seal, his feet resting on the ledge. He was chilled by the cold breeze and felt himself shiver, wondering if it was not more tension than cold. He looked down on the lighted plaza below. Thank God it was late at night and no people about. The court house and library across the plaza were dark. But there was still traffic on Second South Street to the west and Fourth South Street to the north, headlights moving in both directions. Far to the north, over the roofs of office buildings, he could see the golden, life-sized statue of the Angel Moroni on top of the Salt Lake Temple, all lit up. He could barely make out the long trumpet at the angel's mouth, ready to sound the second coming of Jesus Christ.

"It's kind of pretty out there, don't you think?"

Douglas looked over the city as if he had just become aware of its existence. "Yes, it is pretty."

"Can you see the Temple?" Jerry pointed in the direction.

"Yes, I had hoped someday to take both Nancy and Rachel through the Temple. I understand it is very beautiful inside."

"It is beautiful, you would like it. Who knows, someday you, Nancy and Rachel might see the inside for yourselves."

"I doubt it," he lamented. "Not now."

Jerry asked, "Have you thought there might be a reason why you were caught? After all, you didn't pull the trigger, all you did was provide the transportation. That makes quite a difference. Look at it this way, somebody needs to tell the whole story about Phillip and expose him for what he is. Have you stopped to consider that only you can bring out the truth and save the rest of the people who have trusted Phillip. Douglas, as one Mormon to another, I know that God does not want you to jump. It is colder than a witch's tit out here, come back in where it's warm."

They talked for an hour while Mike fidgeted and fretted and paced back and forth, muttering, "That little bastard, if he jumps I'll kill him."

Finally, Douglas relented and said, "I got to go to the bathroom."

Douglas slid sideways towards Jerry. As he reached the window he got on his knees ready to swing inside when he said, "I don't feel very good," and his eyes rolled back into his head. Jerry grabbed the wrist of his right arm and the collar of his jacket just as he collapsed and his legs and torso slid over the ledge. Jerry was off balance and the dead weight nearly pulled him out the window. He jammed his knees against the wall beneath the window as his right hand slipped from the jacket. He used it as a brace against the window edge to keep from being pulled outside. Douglas dangled, limp and unconscious, ten floors above the cement, held only by the wrist. But Jerry's grip was slipping. "MIKE!" he yelled.

Mike reached out over Jerry and grabbed Douglas by the coat. Other detectives followed, holding on to both Jerry and Mike. It took the combined strength of both men to drag Douglas' limp body over the threshold of the window and safely inside. They lay there by the unconscious body of Douglas Cooper, completely exhausted. Finally Mike said, "Somebody go get some smelling salts, I'm going to kick that little bastard's ass."

Chapter Twelve

ARMED WITH WARRANTS of arrest, Mike, Jerry, and the Salt Lake County Sheriff's Tactical Squad sped toward Easterdale, where covert surveillance maintained a half block from the old stone church had assured Sheriff Stewart that Phillip Compton and his two bodyguards were still inside. For two days detectives had watched as families filtered into town, parked their cars, and hustled inside the church—no one coming out. This concerned the Sheriff. He was afraid Compton had found out he was under surveillance, or worse, that arrest warrants were imminent. In a small town, it was hard to keep things quiet.

They all met at the Sheriff's office to make their plans. Jerry counted five highway patrolman and six of Stewart's deputies besides the ten-man swat team. That made a force of twenty-five counting Mike and the Sheriff, more than enough to make the arrests.

A deputy at the surveillance site called the Sheriff and reported that every few minutes more cars arrived with families loaded down with luggage and blankets, making a beeline for the old church. Sheriff Bud Stewart hung up the phone. "They know something is up. I'm afraid we've lost the element of surprise."

Mike suggested they set up roadblocks out of sight of the church. The more people inside, the more difficult it was going to be to talk Compton and his assassins outside. The Sheriff immediately deployed the highway patrolman. But to complicate matters, the press had gotten wind that arrests were soon coming and had started arriving in Easterdale.

Piqued by the news, Bud Stewart blurted out, "How in the hell did they find out?"

Although the question was directed to no one in particular, Mike replied, "Someone in Salt Lake tipped them off, it happens all the time." The Sheriff assigned one of his deputies to act as public affairs officer and sequester the media out of the way.

Cops milled around waiting for orders, aware of the precariousness of the situation. The Sheriff's small office in the town hall, designated as the command center, was filled to capacity with a Sergeant from the Highway Patrol, Mike, Jerry, the Sheriff, and his Chief Deputy. They discussed their alternatives. It was not going to be easy and they knew it. Compton might try to hold them off with guns. That was the worst scenario. The best scenario, call Compton on the telephone and ask him to surrender, bringing with him the three shooters of Harold Barnett. But after Mike and Jerry's earlier confrontation with Compton, no one expected that to happen. Furthermore, it was a safe bet that Compton was receiving detailed information by phone from the outside.

All this was taken into consideration as several alternative plans were proposed, but the final decision would have to be made by Sheriff Stewart. Easterdale was his county and his town, he was the boss. Convinced that Compton was preparing for a confrontation, Sheriff Bud Stewart decided to start with the least severe alternative and work his way up.

Karris answered the telephone. When the Sheriff identified himself, Karris demanded to know what was wanted. The Sheriff replied impatiently, "What I have to say is for Compton only. Now go get him."

Seconds later Compton came on the line. "What do you want, Sheriff?"

"I'll put it to you straight, Phillip. I have six murder warrants. One is for you. I don't want any trouble. I'd like you and the others to give yourselves up."

Compton's voice sounded shaky. The Sheriff couldn't tell if it was from anger, fear, or both. He gave Compton the names on the warrants, the three shooters, Buck Jones, and Karris.

"You can't prove a thing," he answered. "Besides, Sheriff, we don't recognize the legality of those warrants." The octaves in his voice kept rising until he screeched, "We have declared our independence from the United States. This compound is now The Federal Republic of Zion. You have no jurisdiction."

"We have plenty of proof, Phillip," the Sheriff scoffed. "We found the car and we have Douglas Cooper in custody. He told us everything. It's over, Phillip. Give yourself up."

"It's not over," he screeched, "You're only doing this because of our religion. This is religious persecution. We won't give up. We will die first."

"Phillip, be reasonable, listen to me—" The phone went dead. The Sheriff immediately dialed back and got a busy signal. He tried five minutes later and still got the busy signal. Glancing at Mike, he said, "He must have the phone off the hook."

"Either that or he's calling out, or someone is calling in," Jerry remarked.

Mike said, "We've got to find out how many women and children are in there."

The troopers had isolated about fifteen men, women, and

children attempting to sneak past them to the church compound. The deputies and troopers herded them over to the Sheriff's Office where they could be interviewed. It turned into a grueling experience. One woman near hysteria said her husband and three children were inside the compound and she begged the Sheriff to let her join them. Another young man, who claimed to be part of Compton's group, said he thought he could talk them into surrendering and asked to be allowed to try. Each person they interviewed, except for the small children, had an excuse for wanting to be with Compton.

At first they tried interviewing the husband and wife together, but that didn't work because of the husband's domination over the wife. He would answer the questions proposed to his wife. They found that when interviewed separately, the wife proved to be the most cooperative and talkative. Thereupon, it was from a large bosomed women that they learned Compton had telephoned all his people instructing them to gather inside the compound, because the millennium was about to begin. Compton's old stone church compound, they were told, would be the only safe place in the land.

"That foxy old son-of-a-bitch," Mike chimed. "The more people he can get inside that church, the harder it will be for us to root him out."

From the interviews, they estimated that as many as thirty-five men, women, and children were inside the compound. Over half they assumed were children estimated to be younger than sixteen. It made for a very bad job.

The Sheriff tried telephoning Compton one more time. On the third ring Compton answered. "What do you want now, Sheriff?"

"Listen to me, I don't want anyone getting hurt—" Compton cut him off, shouting into the phone. "It's too late for that, Sheriff. If anyone gets hurt it will be on your head. I have talked with the newspapers and television and told them you are persecuting us."

"How many are in there, Phillip?"

"Does it make a difference?" he reproached sarcastically, enjoying the harshness of his cutting remark. He knew the gentle nature of the Sheriff, that he preferred the soft approach as opposed to force. The last thing Stewart would want, Compton knew, was another Waco and would do whatever possible to avoid violence. Therefore, the children were more valuable than guns; they were the high stakes in negotiation and he held all the aces. "For your information, there are fifty-three, mostly children. Their safety is on your shoulders, Sheriff."

"Send the children out, Phillip."

"Surely you're joking," and he made a deep cackling sound. "They don't leave unless we all leave. I warn you, Sheriff, if any of your deputies try to force themselves inside, they will be shot. There will be no more negotiating." The phone went dead.

The Sheriff looked at Mike. "I think he just yanked the phone line out of the wall."

Jerry noticed that the pressure was beginning to show on Sheriff Stewart. He didn't envy the responsibility. With dread, the Sheriff said, "I guess we ought to find out how serious Compton is about shooting."

He assigned himself to walk up to the front door and try to communicate with Compton. One of his deputies volunteered to go in his place, but the Sheriff told him, "I don't want your getting shot on my conscience. I'll go."

Wearing a bulletproof vest under his jacket, Bud Stewart approached from the blind side of the church, and worked his way up to the outside wall. He crept under the windows to the solid oak front door. Standing off to the side, he cautiously reached over and tested the handle. It was locked. Then he pounded hard on the door with his clenched fist. He pounded again and was about to strike the door a third time when a rifle slug came tearing through the door. He jumped back, leaning against the wall. The rifle cracked again and two more slugs ripped through the thick oak leaving ragged splinters.

A Sheriff's car screeched to a stop in front of the church and one of Stewart's deputies jumped out, ducking behind the car with his revolver in hand. The church window to the Sheriff's left shattered and someone pumped three slugs into the patrol car. The deputy returned fire at the window, jumped into the patrol car and sped off. The window shattered on the opposite side of the door and two more shots were fired at the fleeing officer's car.

Sheriff Stewart hugged the stone wall until all was quiet. The sun hung over the mountains in the west; it would soon be dark. He was chilled by the cooling air. As he crept back the way he came, he hesitated and ducked under the window from where the shots came. He listened a moment, but couldn't hear anything.

When he was safely out of harms way, the first thing he did was check on his deputy. It was the same young deputy who had volunteered to take his place. Miraculously, he'd escaped without being hit. Stewart cornered the deputy against his car and in a voice mixed with both sharpness and relief, demanded, "What the hell were you trying to do?"

He was a gangly youth in his early twenties with large, calloused hands and a weathered face. He looked out of place, like a transplant from the frontier. He spoke with a deep country drawl. "When I heard them shooting, I was afraid you got hit. I was coming to save you, but when I saw you was alright, I got out of there."

Stewart tried dialing Compton's telephone number again. The line was dead. Compton had deliberately severed all means of communicating with the outside as a buffer against changing his mind. It looked like a standoff was inevitable. They all looked at each other. For the moment there was nothing to do but wait. Compton was in charge and he knew it. As long as he had a church full of women and children, he could sit there and watch TV news reports and thumb his nose. In a day or two he would have worldwide attention.

In his demented mind, Compton rationalized that national attention was nearly as good as taking over the LDS Church. It had taken years for the LDS Church to gain worldwide attention; he would do it in days. He therefore intended to make the standoff last as long as possible. He fantasized that the name, Phillip Compton, would be uttered around dinner tables as frequently as the name of the president of the United States and Elvis Presley. Before the standoff was over, he resolved, the man Phillip Compton, God's defender of sacred laws, would go down in history alongside the illustrious Joseph Smith. He would become even more famous than Jim Jones or David Koresh. It did not occur to him that the media would not perceive him as a great luminary: By his own fallacious words and feckless acts he was perceived by the media as a shrewd and dangerous lunatic.

"TV—news reports!" remarked Mike, snapping his fingers. "Let's shut off his electricity. The son-of-a- bitch is a megalomanic. Let's not let him revel in the standoff."

When night came they could see the flicker of candles through the curtained windows. Without telephones or electricity Compton could only imagine what was going on with the media. He did not know they had already established a twenty-four hour vigil, scrutinizing every move the Sheriff made, the plight of the children their primary focus.

The weight of being in charge was a burden Bud Stewart had not asked for. The media hounded him, demanding to know what he proposed to do to save the women and children? He had no concrete answers to their questions. As each day passed, he awoke each morning hoping that today would be an end to the nightmare. He could make no plans, no offensive move, not as long as the children were inside the compound. Each attempt to negotiate was answered with a bullet smashing through the front door of the church. Compton placed large signs in the windows that read, "Go away, Gestapo," and "We are the victims of religious persecution." A standoff with children as hostages was the worst possible situation for any cop, let alone a small town Sheriff.

The Utah Governor called. The Attorney General called. They all wanted action but offered no solutions. The Governor called again and said he was sending down the Public Safety Commissioner to take over. Sheriff Bud Stewart replied, "I'm the leading law enforcement officer in this county. If you send your man down, I'll send him back."

The governor, not used to having his orders disobeyed, said, "Stewart, if you want to wear that badge another four years, you better do as I say."

Bud Stewart replied, "Governor, when election time comes around next year you can have this badge and stick it up your ass. I have had it with politics. Until then, the people of this county have put me in charge, win or lose. This is my county and I will run it the way I see fit." After the Sheriff hung up the phone, Mike and Jerry applauded.

The standoff was now in its fifth day. Journalists as far away as Japan, England, France, Germany, Italy, and Australia had set up camp around Easterdale. Alcohol, Tobacco and Firearms (ATF) offered their assistance because they heard Compton possessed illegal weapons. The FBI suddenly appeared on the scene and quartered their swat team at the local high school. The Agent in Charge, Bevin Strack, apologized to the Sheriff, tacitly stating Washington had ordered him to assist, but everyone knew what he was really saying. Mike said it best, "That's a polite way of saying, we're taking over."

It was a general conclusion that the only way the FBI

assisted local law enforcement was when you sent evidence to their forensic laboratories for examination. On occasion, an agent might tag along as an observer at a crime scene search or during an arrest; but in cases like the standoff, they never really assisted, they took over.

In an attempt to pacify and not alienate Sheriff Stewart, Strack said the United States Attorney had decided that the constitutional rights of the children had been violated, making it a federal matter. Besides, the whole world was watching. Politicians were using the standoff as publicity fodder; women and children's action groups used it to promote their agenda. Everyone wanted to get in the act, demanding action—but offered no solutions.

Bud Stewart suspected that the governor had unofficially invited the FBI. In his news releases he praised the superiority of the FBI and put words in the Sheriff's mouth, saying he was sure Bud Stewart welcomed FBI support. In reality Bud Stewart was thought to be a Podunk country Sheriff, ill-sorted to handle a sophisticated hostage situation. The FBI, on the other hand, was viewed as the paradigm of virtue, knowledge, and the panacea of all contingencies. It was as though God had endowed the FBI with everlasting omniscience. Therefore, it was presumed they were automatically actuated and intellectually equipped to deal with a fanatical, doomsday Mormon cult. But as a matter of fact, Sheriff Bud Stewart, as unsophisticated as he might appear, was far more capable of handling demented Mormons than a dozen pompous Washington aristocrats.

Bud Stewart, Mike, and Jerry discussed the fiascos of former Utah standoffs involving dissident Mormons. Mike Levine, outspoken as usual, said each time outside cops moved in and displaced the local cops, the confrontation always ended tragically.

Mike, who more than once had assisted rural sheriffs in high profile crimes, was the first to admit there was an illusion that sophisticated city cops had it all together and always knew best.

One of Compton's loyal followers, an insignificant little guy called Elmer, who had earlier tried to enter the compound, asked the Sheriff if he could go in and try talking Compton into giving up. The Sheriff told him no because Elmer was known around town as a fanatic and the Sheriff suspected he would not come back out. But when the FBI heard about Elmer's offer, they felt it was worth a try. So they gave Elmer a cell phone and sent him on his precarious mission.

For a few minutes, while luxuriating under the warm television floodlights, he had the attention of the world. He spoke with quixotic gallantry into the microphones. Yes, he was a member of the Compton polygamist group. Yes, he thought he could rescue the hostage women and children. And the media epitomized Elmer as Utah's example of intrepid chivalry.

When Elmer first approached the Sheriff, it was a ruse in which to join the only people that had ever made him feel important. Now he had a real cause that was no illusion. He knew that he could get inside safely. But instead of becoming one of them, just a nameless, faceless member of a macabre polygamist cult doomed to oblivion, he could go down in history as the valiant knight of justice and liberty, the guy who saved the women and children.

When he crept along the stony wall of the church towards the front door, ducking underneath windows, a telescopic camera followed him. He was filled with the urgency of his mission and bubbled with passion. Like the infamous Don Quixote, he advanced fearlessly, oblivious of consequences.

When he reached the front door, he called out, "Phillip, it's Elmer, let me in." And then he turned and smiled for the hidden cameras.

He called out again, "Phillip, it's me, Elmer. It's okay, let me in."

Mike, Jerry, and Sheriff Stewart watched with skepticism from behind a car. The Sheriff said, "I hope for Elmer's sake he pulls it off." The Sheriff had made it clear to the media that this was an exclusive FBI operation.

The door opened and Elmer slipped in. The elated FBI agents gave each other the "high five" as if success was just a matter of time. And then the waiting began.

The clock ticked off five minutes, then fifteen. The anxiety level rose with each minute. Bevin Strack dialed the cell phone he had sent in with Elmer. It rang and rang and then the voice message activated. "I am sorry, I cannot come to the phone at this time. At the sound of the tone, please leave a message."

On the half hour, worry started to show on the ruddy face of the Special Agent in Charge. "These things take time," he said. "You can't expect results right off the bat. This could take as long as three or four hours."

An hour went by, and then an hour and a half. Jerry was munching on a sandwich when the front door of the church opened and Elmer came staggering out, obviously pushed. He was without his jacket and his face was puffy red with welts. He tottered a few feet nearly falling when the cell phone he'd been carrying came flying through the air after him. He was dazed and wobbly, having difficulty walking. He had traveled about forty feet, near the street curb, when a shot rang out from one of the windows and Elmer collapsed.

Jerry threw down the sandwich. Mike yelled, "They shot him!" Sheriff Bud Stewart trained his binoculars on the fallen man. Mike asked, "Is he dead?"

"No, it looks like he was hit in the thigh. Just a minute. He's trying to crawl, but he's not making much headway."

"Let's go get him," Mike said angrily.

"Hold it," Jerry cautioned, "that may be what they want us to do."

Sheriff Stewart, Mike, and Jerry sprinted over to where the agent in charge, Bevin Strack, was in deep discussion with his swat team dressed in their bulletproof vests and black coveralls. Strack motioned for them to come in close. He said, "We're going in after him."

"How?" Sheriff Stewart asked, indicating that he was in agreement.

"The team will keep them pinned down in the windows while two men in a car pull up and drag him out."

Mike interjected, "You know, don't you, that they plan to pick us off when we try to grab him?"

While they talked, Jerry examined the front of the building. The chapel was in the right wing, the kitchen and banquet hall in the left wing. The shot that felled Elmer came from the chapel. The thick beige curtain was still pulled aside. Jerry suspected that whoever shot Elmer was still watching, but from far inside and at an angle directly in line with the window, and Elmer. Therefore, the cover fire during the rescue, he suggested to the others, should be directed at that same angle as well as perpendicular to the window.

Elmer attempted to crawl to a gully near the road. A second shot rang out from the window. Chips of sod flew over Elmer's outstretched arm. The muffled sound confirmed Jerry's suspicions that the sniper was deep inside the chapel and not close to the window. An FBI agent yelled at Elmer through a bullhorn. "Don't move, we'll be there in a second."

It was decided that two vehicles would be used as shields, parked at right angles to the window. The FBI Swat Team would take one window and the Sheriff's Swat Team would take the other window. Each team would send a burst of fire into the respective windows just before the rescue car approached Elmer. Strack calculated the operation would take less than a minute.

Strack gave the signal and two autos screeched to a stop at right angles to the windows. Four swat team members armed with assault rifles bailed out, taking positions behind the vehicles. So that everyone inside the church could hear, Strack warned over the bullhorn, "We will be shooting inside the windows. You have ten seconds to clear the windows. Clear the windows or you will be shot. You now have six seconds to clear the windows."

The first burst was aimed deliberately high. Two men concentrated fire directly into the windows while the other two angled their fire over Elmer into the opposite window. The second burst was waist high with the intent of taking out anyone stupid enough to return fire.

The rescue car skidded to a stop on the frosty turf between Elmer and the church. While several more rounds were pumped into the windows, a burley agent in the back seat jumped out, grabbed Elmer, and the car sped away, the back door still open. The operation went off smoothly with no shots fired from the church.

Inside the chapel, Karris lay in a pool of blood. One slug tore his throat open and another passed through his chest. Buck Jones covered his lifeless body with a blanket. In the other wing, a bearded man named Becker moaned as a woman bandaged his shoulder.

Strack bent over Elmer while a paramedic examined the bullet hole in Elmer's thigh. His left eye was swollen shut, a deep gash over the cheek bone. His right eye and lips were puffy and he had difficulty speaking.

"Who worked you over?" Mike asked.

"Buck held me while Karris beat me." His breathing was erratic and he slurred his words, obviously in great pain. "I think my ribs are broken."

"Why did they beat you?"

"Said I was a traitor for wanting to save the women and children. I'm sorry, I really tried," he gasped. Strack placed a comforting hand on his shoulder. Responding to the tenderness, Elmer looked into his eyes and mumbled, "Phillip's gone mad."

The paramedic interrupted. "We have to get him to the Delta City Hospital as soon as possible. I'm going to give him a shot of morphine." He glanced down at Elmer. "It will knock you out."

Elmer raised a hand, gesturing to the paramedic to wait. He turned towards Strack and with great effort said, "Phillip said they all have to die. He said it was Masada all over again."

"Do you know where they're keeping the children?" Strack bent closer to Elmer's mouth. The poor man was getting weaker by the second.

"In the rec-hall by the kitchen."

"How many?"

"Fifteen or more."

Jerry noticed that in spite of his pain, Elmer had a queer look of contentment on his face. Jerry suspected that in Elmer's mind, he savored the compassion he was receiving from these important law enforcement men. It made him feel like he was one of them. The FBI men had made him believe that he was really somebody of value, and no matter what happened in the future, he was glad for what he had done.

The medic inserted the syringe into his shoulder and in seconds Elmer was asleep. They covered him with a blanket, strapped him in the Gurney, and rolled him out to the waiting ambulance.

Chapter Thirteen

THE COFFEE WAS hot and bitter. Strack entered the office. "Washington is sending out a hostage negotiator. He'll be here sometime tomorrow morning."

"How's he going to negotiate?" Mike poured Strack a cup of coffee.

"I don't know at this juncture, but we got to figure out a way to get those kids out of there. This is the fifth day and I'm getting dumped on from the top down. The President is coming down on the Attorney General who is coming down on the Bureau, and that doesn't include the Senators and Representatives."

"I know the feeling," the Sheriff condoled. "I'm getting my share of pressure from the Governor."

There was a knock on the door and a deputy walked in holding a page that had been torn from a magazine. He handed it to Stewart. "This was dropped out the women's restroom window."

It was a page out of a magazine. In the margin was a message, presumably from a woman inside the church. The Sheriff read it so all could hear, "Children escape tomorrow, kitchen door, be ready."

Mike slapped the Sheriff on the back. "It sounds like there's a lady in there that's going to solve our kid problem. Why don't we concoct a diversion to help her."

Strack asked, "What do you have in mind?"

"Let's have your negotiator try and make contact at the front door. Maybe it will pull everybody out of the kitchen and give her a chance to get the kids out the back door."

The Sheriff added, "We can sneak a cell phone up and set it by the front door. I doubt Compton will take it, but it's worth a try."

Strack sneered at the Sheriff. "We can also blast the front door open, lob a tear gas grenade in and send in the swat team. That ought to be plenty of diversion."

"And what about casualties?" asked Mike.

Unsure if Strack was serious or just being sarcastic, Jerry said, "The Sheriff's right, negotiation has to be our first option. Too many things can go wrong if we storm the place."

Visibly perturbed, Strack turned and faced the Sheriff, but he spoke to everyone in the room. "This is now an exclusive FBI operation. Sheriff Stewart, your role is support only. That goes for you too, Mike, you can call your boss for conformation." He looked at Jerry. "Carmichael, you can stay if you want, but keep out of the way."

He started toward the door and hesitated. "I'll decide tomorrow if there is to be a diversion."

Once Strack was gone, Sheriff Stewart asked, "What the hell got into him?"

"It's the guy coming from Washington," volunteered Jerry. "Strack's starting to cave from the pressure. When this guy arrives tomorrow, Strack will have to assure him that the FBI is in control."

"I wouldn't want to be in his shoes," Mike added. "Under normal conditions, he's a pretty good guy. He's been ordered to bring the standoff to a climax, but if it turns badly, he knows it'll be his head that rolls. Uncle Sam doesn't want another Waco."

At 0900 the next morning the hostage negotiator, a swarthy well-dressed man of Italian extraction, arrived on the scene. He was introduced as Agent Costello. They went through the customary handshaking ritual and then Strack and Costello withdrew to plan the next move. Twenty minutes later they returned and handed out assignments. Sheriff Stewart and the Sheriff's Swat Team would visibly support Costello at the front of the church while Costello attempted to make contact inside. A cell phone was placed at the foot of the front doors. The FBI Swat Team was at that moment taking clandestine positions at the rear near the kitchen doors. Stack would join them. The operation would commence in ten minutes. Mike couldn't resist a tad of sarcasm, "Good plan, Strack."

Three sheriff's cars pulled to a stop across the street from the church. Costello and the deputies took positions behind the vehicles. There was a slight movement of the curtains in the church window. Costello balanced the bullhorn on top of the car.

"Phillip Compton, this is Special Agent Costello speaking. I have just arrived from FBI headquarters in Washington D.C. I have a message of great importance. We have placed a cell phone at the foot of the front doors. Please take the phone so we can communicate. We will hold our fire. The message is of great importance."

The media, cordoned a half black away out of sight, knew something was about to take place when they glimpsed the cars take position in front of the church. Their suspicions were confirmed when they heard Costello on the bullhorn; and they commenced hounding the public affairs men for information. For nothing better to do, Jerry stayed close to Mike who was with Costello.

Five minutes passed and nothing happened, so Costello repeated his message, emphasizing the importance that they communicate. The cool breeze out of the south suddenly increased to gusts and clouds began to streak in from the northwest. Three more minutes passed. Mike whispered to Jerry, "Would I like to be a fly on the wall now."

Sheriff Stewart said to Costello, "Keep trying. I suspect Compton is thinking about it and we need to keep his attention here in front."

The bullhorn once again broke the silence. Halfway through the message, Strack's voice blurted excitedly over Costello's hand carried radio. "They're out, they're out, thirteen kids, a man and a women."

One of the doors of the church slowly opened, an arm stretched out and grabbed the cell phone, the door closed with a slam. Costello quickly dialed the cell phone. Inside the church, the phone rang twice and was answered by an acrid male voice.

"This is Phillip Compton, what is it you want?"

"A peaceful settlement," answered Costello.

"Then go away and leave us alone."

"You know we can't do that."

For a few seconds the phone went silent and Costello was afraid he had lost contact. Then Compton's bitter voice reeking with hate said, "By now you know that two cowards have fled with the children. There will be no more cowardly acts."

"Listen to me," Costello pleaded. "There is no need for violence. Let's work out a deal."

"There will be no deal," Compton replied ominously. "It is out of my hands. The millennium is underway. This is the beginning of persecutions and God will soon take vengeance upon you and this wicked generation. We will soon be lifted up by the Almighty and will return with the Son of Man more powerful and brighter than the sun, armed with swords and bolts of lightening, and then we will cleanse the Earth of all wickedness. You have been warned."

Seconds later, the front door opened and the cell phone came sailing out onto the frosty lawn.

Chapter Fourteen

AS THE SKY TURNED black, Sheriff Stewart predicted that a colder, fiercer wind from the north would bring snow.

After the FBI finished interrogating the man and woman who escaped from the church, they turned them over to the Federal Marshal who was waiting to transport them to the County Jail in Salt Lake City. The children were turned over to Child Protective Services and waited disposition. Sheriff Stewart was not permitted to talk to them. It wasn't until he threatened to call FBI headquarters and notify the press that he was finally apprised of the results of the interrogation. With a deliberate show of temper, he said to Strack, "This is

still my county and my town. I'm tired of being treated like
Barney Fife. You federal guys want our cooperation, but you
don't want to share your information with us. I want to know
what is going on or I'm holding a press conference on FBI
arrogance and bad manners."

"Okay," Strack said, "you want to know what they said?
Karris is dead and another man is severely wounded. They got
it when we rescued Elmer. Both the man and woman said it was
Compton's intention to take as many of us as they can before
God reaches down and snatches them up into heaven." And
then his voice trailed off, becoming less belligerent. "There is
talk of mass suicide. That's why the man and women got all the
kids out. Elmer may be right about another Masada."

A mental picture of the ancient Israeli mountain fortress
popped into Mike's mind. He had visited Masada while in
Israel and saw for himself the remains of the earth ramp the
Roman's had built to assault the 2000 foot mountain top. The
zealot Jews, led by Eleazar ben Jair, had held off the resolute
Romans two years. But when the Army crested the fortress in
AD 73, they were surprised to find no resistance. Rather than
be taken captive, 993 Jews—men, women and children—in
lots of ten, chose to take their own lives rather than be
captured.

Jerry took Mike by the shoulder. "We need to talk to the
man and woman before the Marshall leaves." The prisoners
were being held in the mayor's office. Jerry prevailed upon
the Marshal to give them a few minutes with the prisoners.

The woman, in her early twenties, wore a simple cotton
dress. Her long brown hair hung loosely around her tear-
streaked cheeks. She wore no makeup and her eyes were red
from crying. The man stood with his head lowered. Like the
woman, his hands were cuffed to a leather belt around his
waist. He was in his mid-thirties, wearing blue jeans and a
long-sleeved, checkered cowboy shirt. Jerry pulled up two
chairs so the prisoners could sit down.

Mike told them that their heroics in saving the children would not go unnoticed and that he was confident everything would work out in their favor. Jerry wondered how they felt about deserting Compton, but was more concerned with the mood of those inside and how Compton was holding things together.

They were husband and wife. The woman did most of the talking. She apologized profusely, "We're terribly, terribly sorry for participating in Compton's fraud. We've only been members for three months. We used to be part of the Grass Valley Group but left because of the corruption and one-man rule. We were looking for whoever had the keys when we investigated Compton's group. They appeared to be a young, progressive organization with lofty goals, so we decided to give it a go. Once we were accepted, things started happening and before we knew it we were caught up in the standoff. It wasn't until then that we discovered that Compton was behind the murders of the Barnett brothers. We were shocked and afraid to say anything. But when Compton started talking about suicide, we knew exactly what we had to do, get out of there."

Her husband looked down at the handcuffs around his wrists. His brown eyes came up slowly and met the eyes of his wife. "Two of the children are our's. When we got alone we made a plan. I volunteered me and Mary to comfort and quiet the children while the shooting was going on. They were scared to death. Phillip told them the FBI wanted to kill them. It was my wife, Mary, who slipped the message out of the ladies restroom. We hoped and prayed someone would be watching because we were afraid if we suddenly burst out the kitchen door, one of the cops might mistakenly shoot us."

Mary said, "When the FBI offered to negotiate, we hoped it was a signal for us to slip out the kitchen door. There were two armed men guarding the kitchen entrance. When the man started talking on the loudspeaker, the two men asked Clyde to keep an eye out while they went up front to see what was going on. It was all the time we needed. The children had no idea what was going on. We each took a child under our arms and herded them outside. I was never more frightened in my life." Tears gushed from her eyes. "I was more afraid of Compton and his maniac bodyguards than I was the FBI."

Jerry asked them if it was doctrine or the thrill of the adventure that unified the people. The woman said, "Mostly it was the keys. Everyone wants to believe Phillip has the keys. He would tell them over and over, 'we're the only people on earth living all of God's laws.' And he was the only man on earth with the authority to offer the ordinances that would guarantee a place in the celestial kingdom. All he asked in return was allegiance, trust, faith, and tithes, and he could promise that our calling and election would be made sure."

"So they just turned their lives over to him!" Mike asked.

She squirmed on the chair, pulled her hands away from Clyde and wiped the tears on her cheeks. "Conformity," she said, "seemed a fair price to pay in exchange for an exalted place in the next life. He made all our decisions, assumed all responsibility, all we had to do was obey."

Clyde spoke up and said, "It wasn't until we were trapped inside the church that I realized that by following him without question, he turned us into outlaws. It was not our decision to kill the Barnetts or do battle with the police. The next thing I knew, Mary and I were accessories to murder and insurrection."

"Didn't anyone try to talk some sense into Compton or stop him?" Jerry asked Clyde.

"After what they did to poor Elmer? I wasn't about to say anything and get myself beat up. I looked at the faces of the others and they were in complete agreement with Phillip. You have to realize, we were still pretty new in the group and not as brainwashed as the others. When they shot Elmer, it was like a red hot iron in my stomach. I asked myself—What am I doing here? Then it finally hit me. God doesn't expect blind obedience. God doesn't want us to place our minds in the hands of another man. Phillip had no authority. I could finally see it and I had to do something before it was too late." He looked at Mike. "Is it too late?"

"No, it's not too late. We're very glad you and Mary were inside there to get those kids out."

"You know what?" Clyde said. "I've decided the greatest evil one man can do to another is to *knowingly* deprive him of free choice."

Jerry handed Mary some tissue. "I can't understand how Compton can think suicide is a solution to anything."

"This may be hard to understand," he replied. "Phillip convinced us all that it was God's plan for the True Church of Christ to be the spark that ignites the millennium. The whole world, he said, would watch and the little town of Easterdale would become the center of Zion. He said the United States Government would finally be seen as the persecutor of God's prophets. But it was imperative that he and the others not be captured, because they would be put on display like animals in a zoo. He said the honorable and scriptural solution was suicide, only then would the impact of our cause be broadcast around the world. He said we would be famous and ranked alongside the heros and heroines of Masada. He said God had revealed to him that we were to go meet the Savior on the other side of the veil where we all would be glorified, and then would return with Jesus to take up the battle and cleanse the earth for the millennial reign. Phillip described how he would personally march into LDS Church headquarters and zap general authorities left and right.

Chapter Fifteen

NIGHT APPROACHED and dark clouds billowed in from the west. The smell and feel of snow chilled the air. Strack and Costello agreed with each other that they needed to act fast. Stewart was surprised when they asked him for support. The Sheriff warned Strack that by assaulting the church, it would give Compton no other choice but to carry out his suicide pact. Stewart suggested they wait and attempt further negations. Hopefully something would happen to change their minds. They had nothing to lose if they waited a few more days.

According to Clyde and Mary there were at least fifteen men and twelve women left in the house. The three who killed Harold, Marvin, and Hilda were among them. Clyde said they were all well armed with machine pistols and assault rifles and had plenty of ammunition. Mary reminded Clyde they even had gas masks.

Agent Costello said, "It's my opinion we need to try the assault before the suicide becomes a reality. Our guys are well trained and with a little luck we can neutralize Compton and Jones before they start shooting their own people. Tear gas has a way of changing people's minds."

Jerry said, "But as soon as you lob tear gas grenades inside the church, won't that confirm what Compton predicted, all out war with the government?"

"I agree," Stewart remarked. "These people are brainwashed. I'm afraid they will interpret the assault as a kill or be killed scenario."

But Costello and Strack stuck to their plan. "I can't just stand idly by and let them kill each other without lifting a hand," Strack said. "If we can take out the ringleaders, the others might lose faith. An assault is inevitable. I think we have a better chance of saving some of them with an assault than trying to talk some sense in that nut case."

It was decided that the initial assault would be made through the kitchen door in the back. After the church was filled with tear gas, if they moved fast enough, maybe those inside wouldn't have time to put on gas masks. It was essential that every room be filled with tear gas. The effects of the gas *might* shatter their fantasies and change plans. They knew that success was uncertain and casualties on both sides were probable.

Sheriff Stewart said, "I don't think it's worth getting men killed if the gas don't work. I don't expect my men to charge into a hail of bullets. You mark my word, Compton will try and kill as many of us as he can before they take their own lives

Mike whispered to Jerry, "The FBI thinks they, and their ideas, are superior to anyone else. It don't do any good to talk, they're going to do what they damned well please. If we're going in, gas'n the place is a good idea, but I'm not in a hurry to confront a bunch of fanatics with machine pistols." Jerry shared his sentiments.

Stewart said, "Strack, you need to know now, if we encounter return fire, I'm not sending my men inside."

Strack answered. "The way we got it planned your men won't have to go inside."

A map of the church was laid out. Looking at Sheriff Stewart, Costello said the FBI would enter by the kitchen and take one room at a time, pushing the belligerents into the hall, and ultimately into the chapel, or out the front door. With no electricity and the rooms full of gas, visibility would be minimal. Stewart and his deputies were asked to guard the windows and front door and not enter the building. That way, in the dim light, they wouldn't have to worry about shooting each other. He estimated it would take fifteen minutes at most to accomplish the mission.

Jerry thought to himself—In five minutes Compton and all the rest could be dead.

The wind had died to occasional puffs. Spotlights lit up the windows and doors of the church. Snowflakes the size of quarters drifted through the beams.

Men dressed in black flak-jackets kicked open the kitchen

door and two tear gas grenades were rolled inside. One came flying back out, gas sputtering from the capsule. More grenades were lobbed into the windows of the two wings, the bathrooms, and the classrooms at the rear of the building. Gunfire from inside erupted and bullets splintered the wooden front doors and sent the heavy window curtains swaying. Compton and his gang were shooting at every opening from which a man could enter.

Another grenade was rolled into the kitchen, and a gray cloud of gas poured out the doorway. Two agents clad in bullet-proof jackets and gas masks stood back from the door, pointed their assault rifles inside and touched off several rounds. Then two more agents darted into the doorway, guns blazing. They were instantly cut down by return fire. Both men collapsed in the doorway. The other two agents sprayed the inside of the kitchen in every direction and then pulled the two wounded men outside. There was no return fire. The two injured agents had received bruising hits on their jackets and flesh wounds to their legs.

Tear gas was billowing out windows of the church. A layer of wet snow covered the hats and shoulders of the officers waiting near the front door. Gunfire could be heard from inside the church. The agents again sprayed the kitchen with rifle fire. Still no return fire. Two more agents darted inside and hit the floor firing in the direction of the hallway. Still no return fire. Slowly they stood up, moving slowly in the gaseous fog. When they reached the door to the hall, they peeked around the threshold. Candles stuck to dinner plates flickered in the clouds of gas. The candles had been placed on the floor at the entrance to each class room. Not a soul was in sight.

The agents were unable to communicate by radio while wearing the gas masks, so they advanced with hand signals. They bunched around the entrance to the hallway, reluctant to step in the hall for fear it was an ambush. The leader stuck his rifle around the jam and touched off several rounds. There was no return fire. He sent more rounds down the hallway. Candles flipped in the air.

The agents could hear the popping of small arms in the chapel. It suddenly dawned on them what was taking place. They entered the hallway moving as fast as they dared. The first two classrooms were empty. The popping was still coming from the chapel. The leader's heart sank, he felt sick. He sent one of the men back outside to tell the others that they were at the front door and not to shoot when they opened it. He moved beyond the front door, tear gas swirling in his wake. He stepped on a lighted candle so he would not be silhouetted. Behind him, the other agents checked each room, opening windows as they went. When the leader reached the chapel entrance, he snuffed out the remaining candle with his foot. The shooting was still going on inside and this time a bullet splintered the wall beside him.

He peeked around the corner and was narrowly missed by more bullets. Other agents hunched beside him. They knew the suicide slaughter was taking place just a few feet away—and they were helpless to do anything about it.

In a matter of seconds the shooting stopped. The leader carefully peeked around again. The tear gas was so thick he couldn't see the raised dais and pulpit. Nothing happened. He scanned the rows of wooden benches in the swirling, gray darkness. He saw the flash and crack from a rifle at the rear of the chapel. Wood splintered near his face, and he ducked back into the hallway. All was silent. And then they heard the muffled sound of a single shot. Then dead silence.

All the doors and windows were quickly opened. The electricity was turned back on and fans were placed throughout the church except for the chapel. Snowflakes following the air currents through the open front doors began to cover the carpet in the foyer. Pockets of gas stubbornly resisted the fans and clung to fabrics and carpets like a gray mist. But with the electricity back to normal and the aid of four cell flashlights, the officers were able to inspect the grisly scene. The agents, still wearing gas masks, viewed the carnage. The grim details were easy to reconstruct. After the swat team had examined each body for signs of life, Sheriff Stewart, Mike, Jerry, and Costello were permitted to view the carnage.

The corpses were scattered about the raised platform that faced the rows of oak benches. Corpses were sitting in the cushioned chairs, others sat on the floor, their backs to the walls. The faces of most were still covered with gas masks. They lay in contorted, grotesque bloody heaps, one on another, the masks creating an alien insect-like appearance in the gaseous gloom. The macabre scene was chilling even to Mike, a seasoned homicide detective. Of the many mutilated and bullet-riddled cadavers he had witnessed over the years in various stages of petrification, there was nothing to equal the horror of this mass suicide. He wondered if the Romans, when they breached Masada, felt the same squeamish sensations.

They found Phillip Compton slumped in the bishop's chair. The gas mask had been torn from his face exposing a bullet hole between the eyes, the back of his head was matted mush. Jerry studied Compton's death expression. It was not the calm, puttied and powdered sleeping visage of human remains in a casket—but the round-eyed, open-mouthed look of a shocked man confronted by the unexpected. Jerry wondered if his countenance reflected his first glimpse of the other side and the dreadful torment that awaited him.

He was flanked by the crumpled bodies of two of his five wives, their long disheveled hair and arms hanging, their breasts splattered with blood, apparently preferring a bullet to the heart than the head. Buck Jones was easy to identify, the hulk of his back against the wall, legs and feet spread into the aisle, the top his head blown away. The gas mask, and pistol he placed in his mouth, lay in his lap. It was everyone's guess that Buck had been the "grand reaper," dispatching Phillip Compton, his wives and then himself after taking one last shot at the Swat Team.

Jerry tried to visualize the grisly scene of Buck Jones in the vaporous chapel, his tall, murky, bear-like figure moving deliberately from one waiting gas-masked form to another, pointing the pistol with outstretched arm, the flash, the jerk of the body as the head snapped back, and the crumple of flesh and bones and flowing blood. What were they thinking those last few seconds while they waited their turn, hearing the shots going off around them?

Karris's corpse lay beneath a blanket between the oak benches midway in the chapel. It would take a while to identify the shooters of the Barnett boys. In all, the human carrion consisted of eighteen women and fourteen men between the ages of eighteen and sixty-five. Of the thirty-two dead only five, including Compton, Jones, and Karris, were without gas masks. Three, like Jones, had taken their own lives, indicating that Jones the reaper had help from two others.

Jerry watched as Mike moved from one corpse to another, apparently detached from the horror. Mike was going about his business with the objectivity of a pathologist, as he should be. But Jerry could not shake loose the emotional impact of the carnage and wasted humanity. He vacillated between abject pity for the dead and intense revulsion. He hated Compton, even in death, for what he had done to the others. He hated the ugliness and destruction and demonic spirit that hung like a cloud. Never before had Jerry felt the presence of evil so strongly. He couldn't wait to get out of there.

But there was still the matter of the murder of Brigham Arthur Beal. It was Mike's problem now. The suspects had been narrowed down to either Richard Partridge or Leatherbury. Mike was more than qualified and would flush out the culprit. Jerry was grateful to leave it in his hands.

Chapter Sixteen

BETH SAT ON THE wooden bench of the foyer in the Red Lobster Restaurant near the Fashion Place Mall. Her reverie was terminated by Katherine's arrival. With her was an attractive lady of thirty wearing a crimson beret positioned jauntily atop dark brown, short-cropped hair. She was wearing slacks, a cream-colored blouse, and a hot pink scarf around her neck. She was a big-boned girl, but that only enhanced her uniqueness. Her bohemian flair, Beth thought, would whet curiosity and stimulate men to sneak a second glimpse.

Katherine introduced her as Madeline, Parley P. Leatherbury's oldest daughter. Beth was pleasantly amazed at Madeline's appearance. She had obviously spent a few hours roasting in a tanning salon, not the typical pastime for a polygamist daughter.

"I thought you would like to meet Madeline," Katherine said, "you both have something in common."

"And what might that be?" Beth took Madeline's outstretched hand, returning the warm friendly smile.

"You both have this obsession about saving me from the horrors of a polygamist life."

Katherine asked Madeline to tell her story.

"To begin with," Madeline started, "that I left the polygamist life style is not unique. In Harold's AJC, fifty to sixty percent of the females and seventy-five percent of the males leave as soon as they are old enough to go out on their own. Many more women leave after they get a taste of the routine and submissive day-to-day tedium, like me."

Madeline was the oldest of eleven daughters from five mothers. She seldom saw her father while growing up except at church, and of course, when he got hungry for her mother's body and home cooking. Madeline's life revolved around the authority of the priesthood, and the priesthood dictated what she could wear, read, listen to, and who could be her friends.

Madeline said that all her childhood training in church, the girls' classes, and the AJC private school was geared to prepare her to be a plural wife. She had not been taught the intimacies of feminine hygiene. She was overweight, bathed only when she felt like it, didn't shave her legs or under her arms, and didn't use deodorant.

Growing up, except for school, her daily routine was tending the younger siblings of all her dad's wives. She said, "We were not allowed to watch television, so I escaped the daily humdrum by reading adventure stories about exotic places. I thought I was ugly, so I married the first boy that showed an interest in me. I was only seventeen, my daily routine was a monotonous treadmill and I wanted off. But when I married, all I did was trade one treadmill for another."

After bearing five children, one after another, Madeline said she became friends with a family of new converts. She was attracted by their vigorous behavior and venturous outlook on life. They didn't dress or talk or act like the run-of-the-mill polygamists. They had fun wherever they went, joking and clowning with each other. Her children played with their children and she was invited to go camping with them. She loved it. Most of the time her husband stayed home, giving one excuse after another. He was so shy that he felt uncomfortable around their feckless behavior. On the one or two occasions he went camping with her, all he did was sit around, sober as a judge, and didn't speak unless spoken to.

"I started going on walks by myself," she said. "It was an escape. While walking I could think clearly and sort things out. After a while I noticed I was losing weight, a happy bonus, so I took longer walks until I was hiking around town five or six miles every day. I called them my fantasy walks. As my weight dropped, I gained confidence and landed a part-time job with a florist. And then the part-time job turned into a full-time job. I cut my hair. I quit wearing those long drab dresses and bought some flashy clothes. And I didn't stop there, I started using perfumes and cosmetics. Slowly I changed from a polygamist lady to a normal mainstream woman. I waited for my husband to say something nice about the change. I wanted to be romanced, taken to a fancy candle light restaurant and then to a motel. He did nothing, absolutely nothing, not even a flower."

"I don't think he knew what to do," Katherine volunteered. "I've met your ex-husband and he is timid by nature. If you looked as foxy then as you do now, he probably felt inadequate around you."

Madeline's cheeks blushed and her eyes sparkled. "Gee, thanks," she said. "I tried tempting him, seducing him, teasing him, but he would not—could not—respond."

Other men, unaware of her background, found Madeline intrepid and saucy. A whole new world opened up. She could not turn back. She packed her bags and, with her children, moved to the northwest where she now had a good job.

Katherine spoke up, "I promised Madeline I was not going to marry Parley or Richard. She said one was as bad as the other."

Beth reached over and squeezed Madeline on the wrist. "You are an extraordinary woman."

"I'm not so special. I have a friend who is ten times more successful than I am."

She said that one of Richard's daughters had been "carefully guided" into Madeline's family. Her name was Helen. She was twenty-five years younger that Parley, more like a sister to Madeline than a mother. Helen was a cute, spunky, intelligent girl with a mind of her own and she and Parley didn't get along. Helen, also blessed with insatiable endurance, left Parley and never turned back.

Helen stayed with friends until she could afford a place of her own. She put herself through school cleaning bathrooms. Now she was a top executive in a thriving corporation.

After Madeline had finished with her stories, Katherine said, "I'm really glad for you and the other lady, but I know I'm supposed to live plural marriage. It won't be with Parley or Richard. I don't know who it will be with. I'm not going to rush into anything. But I do know that when the time is right the Lord will open up the way."

Beth and Madeline frowned with disapproval, causing Katherine to chuckle. "I know you guys really care about me, but you two needn't fret," she said in appreciation. "Look, when and if I marry again, I promise it will be with an incredibly handsome, fabulously rich, charming, giving, caring prince in shining armor riding on a white steed." The tension expelled, they all laughed like mischievous school girls.

Beth changed the subject and asked Madeline, "How did your mother feel when she thought Katherine was coming into the family?"

"If you mean jealousy or something like that—a new sister wife would not have changed things for her. Long ago, my mother resigned herself to the reality that it is her responsibility to support whatever her husband asks, even if it means giving up time to a new wife. Besides, she liked Katherine and Katherine would have advanced their standing in the group."

Her hazel eyes darted over at Katherine. "I'm sorry to be so blunt, but if you have any brains you'll get as far away from my father and Richard Partridge as you can."

Madeline hesitated, and then decided to drop the whole bomb on Katherine. Unable to hide her disgust, she said, "My father lives in a fantasy land, and he's gotten worse. He has my mother believing that all the killings are part of the cleansing that precedes the millennium. He said that God had been using Phillip Compton to pave the way for him, my father, to set the stage for Christ's millennial rein. He predicted that Richard and others would also be eliminated—leaving, of course, my father alone to take up the scepter of power."

Beth observed the wrinkles of stress on Madeline's forehead. It was not easy for Madeline to reveal those dreadful traits about her father, and Beth had no doubt they were true. Nothing that Madeline could say about Richard Partridge or Parley Leatherbury would surprise her. If they were screwing around with Katherine's mind, how many other women were they doing the same thing to?

Beth suddenly remembered what Jerry had said over breakfast. Lt. Levine still had not found the killer of Brigham Arthur Beal and as she listened to Madeline denounce her father, she suddenly felt sick to her stomach. Jerry had said they narrowed the suspects to either Partridge or Leatherbury. Beth glanced at Katherine, her composure grim, and Beth wondered if she too had thought the same thing. Katherine had rejected Parley. If Parley was having visions of omnipotence and had silenced Brigham by slitting his throat, what might he do to Katherine? She excused herself and made a beeline for the pay phone in the foyer. She dialed Jerry's cell phone.

"I'm at the office," he told her.

Beth's voice was shaky and a pitch higher than usual. Jerry sensed the alarm even before hearing what Madeline had said about her father. "I'm scared to death for Katherine," she told him. "Jerry, I just know it's Leatherbury. He's as dangerous as Phillip Compton."

"Follow her home and stay with her until I get there. I'll call Mike."

The women left together, Beth driving alone, Madeline and Katherine following.

Beth pulled into the driveway behind Katherine. Madeline hugged them and said goodby. Her car was parked on the street in front of the duplex.

Inside, the two women sat down. "Did you notice a car following us?" Beth asked. "You know, the one that kept passing us and then would somehow pass us again?"

Katherine thought a minute. "No, but Madeline and I were busy talking. Who would it have been?"

"Oh, I'm probably just being paranoid, after all that Madeline had to say at dinner."

The two women then recounted and examined Madeline's every word. When Beth told Katherine that Parley Leatherbury was a prime suspect in Brigham Arthur Beal's murder, they looked at each other. Call it premonition, hunch or intuition. Whatever it was it struck them both and neither harbored a doubt. It all fit. Katherine trembled at the thought of the mass suicide, and of Parley kissing her, insisting that God had *foreordained* her to be his plural wife.

Wringing her hands, she said, "I'm terrified! What have I gotten myself into? How could I have been so stupid! At the time, it all seemed so simple, the right thing to do. Even after Harold, Marvin, and Hilda were murdered, I still believed the keys were in the group.

The doorbell rang and Beth jumped up. "That's Jerry, I'll get it." The countenance of both girls relaxed.

Beth opened the door. Before her stood Parley P. Leatherbury, his forehead furrowed, the corners of his mouth turned down. He pushed past Beth, demanding. "Where's Katherine?"

He was inside the house before she could recover from the shock. Katherine stood up trembling. "What is it you want, Parley?"

"I've come to take you away." His feet were planted square apart, his steely eyes shifting from Katherine to Beth. This was the first time Beth had seen Leatherbury and he was surrounded by an aurora of evil foreboding.

With gritted teeth, the muscles in his jaws twitching, he approached her. She stood transfixed, unable to move.

Beth yelled, "She's not going anywhere with you!"

With his eyes locked on Katherine, he snarled, "Who is she?"

"I am the wife of Jerry Carmichael and he is on his way over here so you better leave."

He grabbed Katherine. His grip was like a vise. "I'm not going with you," she cried out, trying to yank away from his hold.

"Yes, you are!" He grabbed her by the shoulders with both hands, then looked deep into her eyes. "It's God's will. I suggest you cooperate and no harm will come to you. Where are the children?"

"At the babysitter," she said, trying hard not to show fear.

"Good, we'll get them later."

"Please don't do this," she begged. "I can't go with you."

She felt the pressure of his hands tightening around her arms. "You're hurting me." She tried to push away but he was too strong. And then impulsively, still struggling, she blurted out, "You killed Brigham!"

The grim expression on his face did not change and she knew she was right. "Yes," he said softly with cold deliberation. "It's God's will. Now if you value the safety of your friend, you will come along."

Beth grabbed him by the shoulders, trying to pull him away from Katherine. "Let her go," she yelled in his ear. With one arm, he backhanded her and she stumbled into a chair. Katherine kicked at his shins and tried to knee him in the crotch. Beth leapt to her feet and attacked him from behind.

Holding Katherine with one powerful hand, he grabbed

Beth and threw her across the room, then slapped Katherine across the face. Staggered by the blow, she nearly collapsed. Struggling to gain her senses, the door bell rang and Beth screamed, "JERRY!"

Leatherbury released his hold on Katherine and she fell away, fighting to regain her balance. With one quick sweep he grabbed Beth by the neck, pulled a switchblade knife from his pocket, the blade shot out of the handle, and he held it to her throat just as the door burst open. Jerry froze. All Jerry could see was the four-inch blade under Beth's chin. Leatherbury knew right where to place the point to gain the maximum effect. With one swift thrust upward he could open up the throat and sever the tongue. Beth's mouth gaped open. Leatherbury held her with pit bull tenacity. She was helpless, totally at the mercy of Leatherbury. Beth knew it, Leatherbury knew it, and Jerry knew it.

No words were necessary. It was obvious that for the moment, Leatherbury had the upper hand. He was no longer a saintly apostle. Underneath that ornamental, disarming veneer lurked a ruthless killer. With powerful shoulders and arms, he manipulated Beth with no-nonsense dexterity. Katherine moved between Jerry and Leatherbury, pleading, wringing her hands. "Please, Parley, let Beth go. I will do anything you say. I'll go with you, I'll marry you, anything, just let Beth go."

"Drop your gun!" Leatherbury ordered.

"I'm not carrying a gun." Very slowly Jerry pulled the flaps of his jacket apart so Leatherbury could see he was telling the truth. His .38 lay secure in the glove compartment of his car. Although he had the same police powers as a State Trooper, his job did not require that he carry a weapon at all times. He knew that under the circumstances, he would have had to give up his weapon and then Leatherbury would have been armed with a gun as well as a knife. For once he was glad to be unarmed.

His mind raced and the adrenaline pumped. He felt himself tremble with hate and anger, but fought back the overwhelming impulse to attack. Leatherbury and Beth were at least twelve feet away, and he could not possibly reach them in time to prevent Beth's throat from being slashed. Jerry blocked Parley's path to the front door, holding out his hands in a halting posture. He said, "Let's talk this over before somebody gets hurt," hoping to calm the confrontation. Beth and Katherine were near hysterics. He needed to stall for time. Mike was on his way over and could arrive anytime. But he could tell by the scowl on Leatherbury's face that negotiating was out of the question.

More than once Jerry had talked weapons out of the hands of rapists and deranged convicts. Hostage negotiation had been one of his strong points. But negotiating for the life of his wife? No amount of training could prepare a cop for that. He told himself—Stay calm. He whispered a prayer under his breath, "God help me."

"There will be no talking," Leatherbury shot back. "I want you out of my way or your wife dies. I'm leaving here with Katherine and your wife, and I had better not be followed. Don't underestimate me. I've got nothing to lose." He poked the tender skin of Beth's neck with the blade of the knife showing he meant business, causing Beth to awkwardly raise her jaw. "Please don't take Beth," Katherine pleaded.

"I'll let her go when I'm out of danger."

"Promise!"

"Yes, I promise," he said. "Now let's go."

Jerry's stomach lurched. How could he let Leatherbury take Beth? How could he stop him without Beth getting hurt? *Oh God, what to do?*

"Katherine—you go first." Leatherbury ordered.

Jerry stepped aside as Katherine walked out the front door. Leatherbury and Beth followed, the knife at her throat. Jerry's first thought was to make a grab for his knife hand as they passed, but Leatherbury ordered him to get back. Helplessly, he backed out of reach. As they passed, Beth and Jerry's terrified eyes locked for a split second.

Chapter Seventeen

PARLEY ORDERED KATHERINE to get behind the wheel of Beth's car, then forced Beth into the back seat, climbing in after her, the knife never more than an inch from Beth's throat. The car backed out of the driveway and started down the street.

Jerry could see Leatherbury's arm around Beth's neck through the rear window. The car pulled away, and he had never felt so helpless in his life.

Reaching for his cell phone, he jumped in his car, following in slow pursuit. "Mike," he yelled into the phone, fighting back tears, "Leatherbury's got Beth. Do you have a helicopter in the air?"

Mike confirmed a sheriff's helicopter was at that moment completing a training exercise over the dry farms at the west end of the valley. Jerry relayed the coordinates and description of Beth's car, a teal green Mustang, Utah license: MV4321. The Mustang was southbound on Bangerter Highway. The helicopter estimated contact in two minutes. There were traffic lights at every major junction. Jerry prayed that Katherine would catch every one of them.

The helicopter made visual contact at 5400 South. Jerry dropped back out of sight. He did not have a radio in his car so he rendezvoused with Mike. Together in Mike's car they continued south on Bangerter while maintaining radio contact with the Sheriff's helicopter. Three unmarked detective cars were dispatched to assist. The Sheriff was notified and the Swat Team mobilized. The Field

Commander alerted all available patrol cars, and all cars involved in the soft pursuit switched to the surveillance channel. The Sheriff instructed Mike to call the shots.

The Mustang turned east and then south. At 1700 West it turned north and west again on 9000 South. "He's got a destination in mind and wants to make sure he's not being followed," Mike remarked, glancing at Jerry to see how he was doing. Jerry didn't answer. He stared out the windshield, the muscles in his jaws twitching. "Jerry, we're going to get her back, pal." Mike did his best to sound confident. "We're going to get both of them back and then we're going to hang that bastard up by his balls."

The Mustang pulled over just before approaching 4000 West. "Maybe he's going to let Beth go," Mike said softly.

"I doubt it," Jerry retorted. "He's still trying to find out if he's been followed. If I were him I wouldn't let her go." Mike knew Jerry was right. Leatherbury needed Beth to insure Katherine's cooperation. Mike couldn't bring himself to say anything to Jerry, but he knew, and he was sure Jerry knew, they were going to have to rescue Beth or she was a dead woman.

The Mustang turned south at 4000 West. A second fully fueled chopper with a sniper took off from Airport Number One and headed south. A chopper belonging to a local television station followed a mile behind. Mike instructed the Sheriff's Public Affairs officer to ask all radio and television stations to withhold any broadcasts in case Leatherbury was listening. "That's all we need," Mike said sarcastically, "is for some media asshole to announce to the world we are holding a helicopter surveillance."

The Mustang circled, stopped and started, then doubled back for ten minutes before racing west on Old Bingham Highway. At Utah Highway 111, it turned south and then east on 11800 South and south again to the rural hamlet of Herriman.

Like most small Utah communities, Herriman traced its roots back to the 1850s shortly after Brigham Young piloted the first wagon train of Mormons to the Salt Lake Valley. The sixty odd houses, homes of miners and farmers, were nestled in the southwestern corner of the valley at the foot of the Oquirrh Mountains, surrounded by dry farms and sage brush hills. The massive red and brown tailing dumps from the Kennecott Copper open pit mine overlooked the town. From the air it resembled an oasis of Cottonwood trees with a few houses scattered around the perimeter of trees. Herriman had gone virtually untouched by backhoes and building contractors for a hundred years until the 1980s, when Salt Lake County's population exploded. To the south, angling upward into the mouth of Rose Canyon, subdivisions and prestigious country estates now dominated the dry farms. Because of its isolation, polygamist families had quietly taken up residence in Herriman and probably consisted of a small portion of the population. It was to one of these residences on the northern perimeter of the old section of Herriman that Leatherbury headed.

It was an old yellow brick house with a shingled roof. Ugly curtains covered the windows. The front door looked like it hadn't been used in thirty years. A few bricks had worked loose from the chimney leaving a gapping scar. A wooden platform beneath the back door substituted for a porch.

There was no lawn, just the skeletons of lilac bushes sticking out of the ground and some half- dead apple trees in the back yard. Adjacent to the trees stood a rickety, clapboard shed with a corrugated tin roof frayed by the wind, and a corral made of wooden pallets with three skinny goats. When they pulled up, a flock of black and white magpies flew squawking out of the shed.

Leatherbury ordered Beth out of the car and made Katherine walk in front of them up to the back door of the old house. He lead Beth by the arm, his knife hand at his side. The house smelled of animal grease and cooked meat. Beth had regained some composure and knew in her heart that Jerry was somewhere near. She tried to think what Jerry would tell her to do, what to say, how to act. The only thought that came to mind was stall, get Leatherbury to relax, let him believe she would cooperate.

The back door was not locked. After pushing Beth inside, he bolted the door behind him and herded them through the cluttered kitchen into the musty front room. It was getting dark and he clicked on a corner, upright lamp with a faded green shade and golf ball sized tassels. The light was dim and yellowish, probably a 40 watt bulb. He made them sit on an overstuffed couch next to the lamp. Then he pulled up a cushioned, straight back chair and sat down in front of them.

"What happens now," Beth asked.

"We wait."

"For what?" she demanded.

"For your husband and his friend from the Sheriff's Office, Mike the Jew."

"No one followed us," Katherine insisted. "We would have seen them."

He smiled an "all knowing" smile and didn't say anything in return.

"When are you going to let Beth go?"

"In the morning."

"You promised to let her go when you were out of danger. You're in no danger now."

"Plans have changed. If nothing happens in the night, I'll leave you both here in the morning. You're both excess baggage now. It's too bad Katherine, together we could have made beautiful children."

Beth asked, "Are you really serious about letting us both go." She studied his square face, for the first time noticing the beginning growth of jowls beneath his ears.

"When I leave here in the morning you will both be free as a bird," he replied casually, still grinning slyly.

Beth examined the dingy room, looking for a way to escape. It reminded her of 1940s decor. The floor was carpeted with an old threadbare Persian rug. The furniture was old with bedspreads covering the worn parts. On the floor lay tools. Partially obscured by a chair was the handle of a ball-peen hammer. While Leatherbury peeked out the window, Beth nudged Katherine and pointed towards the hammer. Katherine nodded.

Beth asked if she could use the bathroom. Leatherbury pondered the request and finally said she could. The bathroom was off the kitchen. He told Katherine not to try and leave by the front door, it was nailed shut. He stood in the kitchen near the back door where he could watch both Katherine and the bathroom door. "Dammit!" Katherine muttered beneath her breath. She had hoped to grab the hammer and hide it between the cushions.

The inside of the toilet bowl had turned a rusty color from lack of use. A dead spider floated on the surface. She tried the window, but it was stuck shut with layers of white paint. The medicine cabinet was empty except for an old knotted tube of toothpaste and a bottle of Vaseline Hair Tonic. She had hoped to find a straight edge razor or something else she could use as a weapon. There was only a moldy toilet plunger. She guessed she could jam the wooden handle into his ribs like a sword. Jerry had showed her how police were trained to use a Billy Club. At least she knew it was there if nothing else could be found. She flushed and watched as the spider spun around and disappeared in the whirlpool. When Beth returned to the couch, she noticed the hammer had not been touched. Well, at least there were two known weapons in the house, a toilet plunger and a half hidden hammer.

It was nearly 10:00 P.M. and Leatherbury had established a routine. About every ten minutes he would peek out one of the several windows. There were no street lights and the nearest house was a half block away. Even in the darkness, Leatherbury felt he had a good chance of spotting anyone who sneaked up to the house. When he slipped out the back door for a half minute, Beth suspected it was to urinate as much as to look around.

Katherine was closer to the hammer. She grabbed it and tucked it between the cushions. Then she whispered to Beth, "Do you think Jerry was able to follow us?"

Beth said yes and asked Katherine, "Do you think he plans to kill us?"

"Yes."

They stared at each other. Beth wondered how they could be so frightened and at the same time so calm, as if braced for the inevitable. The faces of Katherine's children flashed in her mind, and then of Jerry, frantic with worry, somewhere outside. *Please, God, let him be there.*

Beth whispered, "There's a toilet plunger in the bathroom. If one of us gets the chance, drive the wooden part into his solar plexus." Just before Leatherbury came back in, they agreed that when he relaxed and got sleepy, if Jerry and Mike hadn't arrived, they would try to escape. They would rather die fighting than be slaughtered like lambs.

A half hour later, Beth stretched and said, "It's going to be a long night," and snuggled into the cushions of the couch. Leatherbury appeared relaxed, both hands resting on his legs, the knife in his right hand.

Katherine studied Leatherbury's face. "Parley," she said, "why don't you give yourself up? You know they won't stop until they catch you, even if you let us go."

He looked at her as though she were crazy. "Never!" he said. "Do you think I would allow myself to be put on display, to be humiliated? GOD will NEVER let it happen. In the morning I will be gone and they will never find me."

"Where will you go?"

"Canada, Mexico. We have people in both places."

"But you killed Brigham."

"Yes, Brigham was expendable. He should have minded his own business." He looked at Beth. "You should have minded your own business."

Beth stiffened at the remark. The expression on his face was dead serious. She touched her upper arm. It still hurt where he had held her while the knife was at her throat. "You'll never get away," she said, "especially if you harm one of us." She had a sudden impulse to plead, *for God's sake let us go.* But she knew it would do no good. She had to remain calm, alert, brave, not show fear, that's what Jerry would say. *Surely he was out there somewhere.* But she couldn't just wait.

"Don't be too sure, my dear," he replied, shaking the knife at her. "You forget, I have the Lord on my side. He will sustain me because of who I am." He looked at the ceiling and his eyes became dreamy as if he were looking at a faraway place. "Where I am, the priesthood will be." His gaze returned to Katherine and Beth. "Phillip Compton was a tool in my hands. Once Phillip eliminated Harold and Calvin, he was no longer needed. The Lord arranged for his suicide. Only the fool, Richard Partridge, stands in my way. But the Lord will soon take him, leaving me to reign unchallenged." His eyes glowed with lust. "I will do what Phillip could not do. I will unite all the fundamentalists under one banner. Then I will assume control of the LDS Church. And if anyone should oppose me, I shall walk over them like stubble. It is foreordained. It cannot be stopped."

Katherine and Beth listened, disbelief and horror masked their faces. Beth thought—he actually believes what he is saying.

Two blocks away, concealed from view by trees and houses, the Swat Team, wearing black jackets, black pants and black-knit ski hats, unloaded their paraphernalia. The Team worked its way through backyards, climbed fences, jumped irrigation ditches until they reached open ground. The going was slow, the footing was hazardous and muffled curses were uttered in the blackness of the night. They made a wide circle in a field of grain stubble, approaching the yellow brick house from behind the goat corral. The bleating goats, at first alarmed, greeted the shadowy figures with flicking tails, in hopes of being fed.

The men received their assignments and dispersed around the house. Mike and Jerry hid behind Beth's car parked by the back door. They were not there more than thirty seconds when Leatherbury stepped outside and took a leak. He stood there, his hand at his crotch, looking in all directions. They barely had time to crouch behind the car and would have taken him then, but they didn't know if more men were inside guarding the girls. To take him now would be risky. Before they could make up their minds, he was back inside.

It was black and cold, below freezing. For an hour they watched and listened. Only one room emitted light, dim at that. They observed curtains pulled back every ten minutes. Between curtain pulls, Mike circled the house looking for an open window, but they were all locked and curtained. Very cautiously he tested the front and back doors. Both were locked. As he went to step off the front porch, a board squeaked. He quickly ducked into a shadow and listened for any sounds coming from the house. There were none.

When Mike returned to the back where Jerry was waiting, he said, "I can't tell how many people are inside, but if there were many I think I would have heard them talking. I think Leatherbury is alone with the girls inside the front room."

The only pattern was the ten-minute window pulls. Mike whispered instructions to the other deputies over the small radios attached to the epaulets on their coats. The men were beating their hands together in the intense cold, anxious to get the job done. Mike beckoned to Jerry. "After the next curtain pull we go in, front and back at the same time." Mike passed the word, "Take out Leatherbury at the first opportunity."

Katherine asked Parley if she and Beth could stand and stretch but he said no, only one at a time. He told Katherine to go first and watched with erotic interest as she raised her arms and purposely thrust out her bosoms. Beth shuddered at the leer on his face.

Katherine stretched tantalizingly a second time, this time provoking him with her buttocks. "I'm thirsty," she said seductively. "May I get a drink?"

Leatherbury grinned, "Sure, and while you're at it, run out the back door. Do you think I'm stupid?"

"I wouldn't do that."

"Sure you wouldn't. I'll get you a drink as soon as you sit back down."

Beth said, "I would like a drink, too."

He laughed strangely, and said, "And I suppose you would hold my knife for me so I could carry both glasses?"

He walked into the kitchen. "Be ready," Katherine whispered.

After filling a tumbler with water, he started toward the front room, hesitated, then walked over to the back door. With his knife hand he attempted to unbolt the door but was having difficulty, the knife kept getting in the way. He looked down at the water glass in his other hand, shook his head with frustration and started back toward the front room.

Katherine stood up to receive the water glass, took it in her hand and sipped. Leatherbury turned to return to his chair when Katherine said seductively, "Oh, Parley."

He was blinded by the water splashing in his face. His knife hand raised automatically. Katherine screamed, "GET OUT, BETH," but Beth was reaching for the hammer between the cushions.

Katherine grabbed his knife arm with both hands and sunk her teeth into his wrist. He cried out from the pain and the knife fell to the floor. Cursing, he grabbed her by the hair and yanked her head away. She yelled again, "BETH, RUN!"

Outside, Jerry and Mike jerked their heads towards the house. "Did you hear that?"

Mike answered, "It sounded like a scream." Mike keyed his radio and said, "Something is going on in the house. We're moving up to the back door. Be prepared to go."

Leatherbury held Katherine in a neck lock and wiped the water from his eyes. His vision cleared just in time to see Beth rushing at him, the hammer raised to strike. He twisted away, pulling Katherine against him as a shield. Beth hesitated, afraid she might hit Katherine by mistake. Katherine tried to break away, but his hold was too strong.

Then he hurled her through the air like a rag doll and she collided with Beth. Both girls screamed as they fell to the ground, the hammer flying free. Leatherbury stood over them, scanning the floor for his knife. Seeing it, he bent to snatch it up when both girls crashed into him, clawing and kicking.

Jerry rushed at the back door hitting it square with his shoulder. It went like slow motion, his mind dazed by the screams. The old door burst off its hinges and Jerry went flying inside, pistol in his hand. He landed on the floor with a thud, rolled and faced the lighted door.

Mike was right behind him followed by two more deputies, guns at the ready. Mike dropped to his knees in the doorway to the front room, poised for rapid fire, holding his pistol in both hands. The other two deputies towered over him, their weapons also trained on the front room.

Katherine and Beth were on the floor, holding each other, sobbing, rocking back and forth. Leatherbury's outstretched body lay on the floor beside them. The side of his head was matted with blood. The hammer lay close by.

Beth looked up through blurred eyes. Slowly, she staggered to her feet and threw her arms around Jerry. He hugged her tight, kissing her hair, assuring her softly that it was all over, all over.

She pulled gently away. Katherine was standing a few feet away, her head bowed. Beth motioned for her to come close. Beth put one arm around Katherine and the other around Jerry, squeezing them all together. They sobbed on Jerry's chest.

Chapter Eighteen

"NO FINGER PRINTS were found on the hammer handle," Mike said, handing the lab report to Jerry. "Maybe he conked himself on the head."

Jerry shrugged his shoulders. "Maybe it's best we don't know which one cracked open his head. I just hope it wasn't Beth."

"Well, I'm not going to push it," Mike said, "and neither is the County Attorney. It really doesn't matter anyway. It was self defense. It's just that everyone is wondering who it was that conked him. In the heat of a fight, when emotions and fear are at their peak, maybe they're telling the truth when they say they don't know who killed him. If only we had been ten seconds sooner, one of us could have done the job for them. How's Beth doing?"

"It's been rough for her. She screams out in her sleep but never really wakes up. I just hold her and tell her she's safe. She and Katherine have something cooked up for tonight. I'm supposed to meet them for an early dinner at the Balsam Steak House."

It took a few seconds for Jerry's eyes to adjust to the dim light. The girls were already seated in a back corner booth. Candles flickered on the table alongside a vase with three red roses. The napkins were a rich wine color. Henry Mancini's rendition of "Mr. Lucky" played softly in the background.

Jerry slid in the opposite side. "What's the occasion," he asked. He had wondered how the friendship between Beth and Katherine would be affected by their ordeal with Leatherbury.

He took a sip of water. "Out with it," he commanded in fun.

Beth spoke first. "I have asked Katherine to join me in organizing a woman's support group. We would assist abused and neglected women and their children in leaving the coercive polygamist cults."

"I don't know," Jerry mumbled, "It's a sticky issue."

"I know it is very political, but our message would be to the women who are caught up in the cults and want to get out."

"What makes you think there are women who would actually leave?"

"Jerry, you must understand my position," Katherine explained. "I'm taking a hard look at my plan to find a polygamous husband after all that I've just gone through. But I haven't made my final decision. . . so what we say tonight is speculation on my part. . . and maybe it's more than speculation. . . . I just don't know yet. But I am willing to share with you what Beth and I have discussed. She has asked me, and I've told her, about the various women I either know or know about who are in a polygamous marriage."

Katherine nibbled on her lip, searching for the right words. "Jerry," she said, "there are three stages where a woman convert might be receptive to help. The first stage is when she is studying the principle but hasn't committed herself. She may be married or single.

"The second stage is where the woman has been in the cult for a year or two and wants out. She would need to know there are people who understand, who aren't judgmental, and who can help her re-establish in society."

Jerry interrupted. "I've been told that in the Barnett Group, men and women come and go all the time without outside assistance."

"Let me give you an example of a story my sister told me," Katherine remarked. "There's a girl named Charlotte. She married when she was seventeen to a man thirty. She was the third wife. She thought that because her childhood friend was the second wife, they would be compatible. But the second wife was the favorite and extremely jealous.

"She got out of that relationship and became the fifth wife in another family where her sister was the third wife. The husband, his name is Kenneth, had a lot of money and was very close to the priesthood leaders. As it turned out, her husband's money was ill-gotten gain. When the law started investigating, Kenneth panicked and turned the stolen money over to another man who ran off to Australia. Kenneth lost everything. So he moved his family into mice-infested trailers out on the west desert. For two years Charlotte and her five children packed water from a tap fifty feet away so they could flush the toilet. She had to gather firewood. In the winter, she and all the children slept in one bed to keep warm. When she complained, Kenneth told her she was crazy and should be grateful he married her, because without his willingness to be her husband, she had no salvation. He then tried to get her to commit herself to a mental institution."

Beth pulled a pencil and notebook from her purse and started writing as Katherine talked.

"She made all the repairs to the trailer because Kenneth was gone most of the time, mooching off friends in Salt Lake.

For two weeks all she and her five children had to eat was bread and water. Finally, she ran off to Ely, Nevada, and poured her heart out to the local welfare board. She returned with food for her children.

"There were several other polygamous families living in trailers around her. The men held a meeting and publicly chastised her for exposing their lifestyle to the welfare people. Then after nothing happened, the rest of the women also went on welfare.

"Charlotte finally had enough. She packed up what little belongings she had and left. The State helped her get established in a small town in central Utah. She went to Snow College, got a degree, and now works as a psychologist in California.

"I'm sure that going out on her own was a frightening thing for Charlotte. Beth's support group idea could have made it a lot easier, saved her time and anxiety."

"Are there many stories like that," Jerry asked.

"My sister, who as you know is a polygamist, told me many good stories and she also told me the bad ones," Katherine explained.

"I've heard enough from Katherine to know there is a real need for a bonafide support group," Beth replied.

"I can see where you could be of help in the first two stages," Jerry said. "What about the third stage?"

"You remember Rachel Heywood, don't you?" Katherine asked.

Jerry nodded.

Beth blurted out, "Every time I think of that pervert, Marvin Heywood, my blood boils. Because of what he did, that beautiful little girl actually considered becoming a prostitute."

Katherine continued, "Beth feels the third stage would be with girls Rachel's age who have second thoughts about polygamy. They watch movies, read books, and see how the rest of the world lives. In the *closed* polygamist societies, the cult leaders shelter the young girls from the world so they won't be influenced. In the Barnett Group, where they have more freedom, thanks to Harold Barnett, many more girls Rachel's age leave the group than stay. But some of the girls are timid or don't have the self esteem to strike out on their own. That's where Beth feels we can be of help and inform them of their alternatives."

Beth spoke up. "Tell Jerry about the teenage girls in the Johnson Group."

"It is taught that the Johnson lineage is a superior blood line and it's okay to marry cousins and half sisters. The Johnson boys, because they are the blue bloods, have gathered the most wives, all pretty young things. The fathers of these girls sometimes coerce their daughters, as soon as they reach the age of copulation, into marrying the Johnson boys for political reasons. There might be ten or fifteen of these young women married to one man. They get lonely and bored, so they sneak out at night and cavort with boys their own age."

Beth took a drink of water and said, "Jerry, I introduced Katherine to Nick Foreman. I heard about him from a friend. For nearly thirty years Nick has been studying the Utah polygamist movement. He knows more about the polygamist history than ninety-nine percent of the polygamists."

"At first I didn't want to talk to Nick," Katherine admitted.

"So what did he tell you?" asked Jerry.

"Nick said that the polygamist justification claimed by the organized groups hinged on the Lorin Woolley story and an alleged eight-hour meeting conducted by John Taylor. You've heard the story, haven't you? Where Joseph Smith was supposed to have appeared to John Taylor and commissioned him to keep the practice of plural marriage alive, because Wilford Woodruff was going to capitulate to the United States Government and issue a manifesto prohibiting polygamy."

Jerry nodded, indicating that he had heard the story.

"Well, Nick was permitted by the LDS Church to examine the diary of John Taylor on the dates that are pertinent to the Lorin Woolley story—September 26 and 27 of 1886. Nick found nothing that even remotely resembled the Lorin Woolley story. In the diary, John Taylor named those men that were present during the sacrament meeting, Sunday, September 26, 1886. Lorin Woolley's name was not among them. You will remember that John Taylor was in hiding from federal marshals at the time." Katherine paused, deep in thought.

Beth continued the story, "Nick also obtained the diaries of George Q. Cannon who was supposed to be at the meeting, and the diary of Samuel Bateman who was supposed to be one of the men set apart to perpetuate plural marriage. Nick said there was, again, nothing in either diary to substantiate the Lorin Woolley story.

"The first account of the Lorin Woolley story did not surface until 1912, twenty-six years after the fact. Don't you find that interesting? Lorin was attending meetings at that time at the Baldwin Radio factory on Highland Drive at about 3300 South Street. Most of the men who first started the fundamentalist underground, Lorin Woolley, Joseph Musser, John Y. Barlow and others, worked at the Baldwin Radio factory. It was at one of these meetings that Lorin first introduced his story. All the people that he named as being present during the eight-hour meeting, the people that could corroborate his story, were dead."

Beth looked at Jerry. "You've been in law enforcement all your life. If you had to go to court with that kind of evidence, hoping to prove the Lorin Woolley story was factual, how far would you get?"

"I'd be laughed out of court."

Beth continued. "Nick did not conduct a flippant investigation, Jerry. It was a long arduous task. As an investigator you should read his book. You'll be impressed with what he came up with, and how he went about it. The book is out of print, but can be found in libraries and will soon be on the Internet.

"As a history of the fundamentalist movement, especially during the underground years, Nick's account is unequaled," Beth said. "Perhaps his book should be read by every man and women considering a polygamist lifestyle."

Jerry nodded. "I read where a new polygamist group has moved into Utah and settled in the little town of Circleville. It's mostly an Internet movement, nothing like Compton's organization. The pastor of this movement takes the position that plural marriage was an Old Testament practice, and nowhere in the Bible does it prohibit polygamy. He calls his movement, Christian Polygamy, and does not claim any supernatural authorization to justify his lifestyle. This pastor insists that polygamy should be a legitimate alternative lifestyle. His position is that where all participants are consenting adults, it can't be considered adultery. And to go one step further, I hear through the grapevine that there is a movement among independent fundamentalists to portray plural marriage as a political choice, just like same sex marriages. They think that under the 14th Amendment, they have a chance."

Beth rolled her eyes and said, "This whole polygamy business makes my head swim."

Jerry replied, "But I think it's rather obvious, no matter what position you take, or from what view you look at it, the practice of polygamy in Utah is not going away. I suspect that if you want to combat polygamy, you should try and educate those people with a propensity towards that lifestyle. Tell them about the pitfalls, and I don't just mean the tough emotional trials, I mean warn them about the human predators and parasites that are waiting to plunder their faith and assets."

"I like Nick's approach," Katherine admitted. "He doesn't judge the fundamentalists or try to humiliate them. He respects their honest opinion. He presents the facts as he has found them, and they can draw their own conclusions. He doesn't condemn them, call them names, any of that stuff. He knows there are a lot of wonderful, intelligent people among the fundamentalists, and he would like them to know what he has discovered."

"Nick Foreman has done a good job," said Beth.

"Katherine," Jerry said, "you are as solid as a rock. Frankly, I just don't see you as a polygamist. . . you just don't fit. Beth and I will give you all the support we can as you try and come to a decision. Meanwhile," Jerry chuckled, "why don't we find you a single, good looking, wealthy Mormon boy to date."

Katherine answered with a smile, "Thanks anyway, but I don't need anyone playing cupid." She paused and looked away. "What I really need, Jerry, is time . . . time to sort all this out. A great deal has happened to me in the past few weeks. Harold was kind-hearted and wanted me to have a choice about my life. He told me to take my time and not be in a hurry.

"Then there was Phillip Compton. Clearly he wanted no one to have a choice of any kind. It was his way or no way and. . . he is as evil a man as I have ever heard or read about. Then, of course, there's Parley. . .a story we all want to put behind us. . .except I still have nightmares. . .where I am actually married to the man. . .."

Jerry grew silent. Faces flooded his mind—Phillip Compton, Marvin Heywood, Richard Partridge, Parley Leatherbury—lusting for power or sex or both. . .letting no one stand in their way. It made him sick to his stomach. Then he smiled, remembering the Grass Valley young lady behind the counter who did not say hello, her bland, unsmiling face offering no hint of her thoughts. . .until he told her the turtle joke, and her cheeks turned rosy and her face stretched into a pretty smile, her brown eyes lit up, and she called after him, "Have a good day!"

Jerry's heart quickened. Where, he asked himself, do most of these women hide their playful little girl selves when they enter polygamy. Does the little girl have to go so deep, for so long, that over time she becomes lost . . . as if she had never lived at all.

A little girl. . .full of fun and excitement. . .suddenly forced into a non-life. . .her vibrant and beautiful energy ground underfoot by the boot heel of some *authority*. . . robbed of who she is. . .never becoming. . .never again hoping, dreaming. . .never again.

Is this what would happen to Katherine—over time. Or to her daughter, or her daughter's daughter. He couldn't bear the thought.

"Ladies, let's get out of here."

Afterword

Both sides of polygamy must be addressed. As an anthropologist, I have often presented the positive sides to plural marriage. Llewellyn, using actual incidents from polygamy's history, creatively presents many of the negative sides. His fiction novel reflects the complexities and vastly diverse experiences inherent in contemporary Mormon fundamentalism.

The media has created a climate of horror and mayhem surrounding polygamy. Stories of child sexual abuse, kidnaping, wife beating, brainwashing, abhorrent living conditions, and murder are just a few of the many sensational headlines one can see any day of the week in the Utah and national press. Yes, abuses occur in polygamy just as they do in monogamy. But there is another side to polygamy equally compelling.

To provide a balance to reports in the media, I present an alternative view. After 10 years of observing polygamy in the Intermountain States region, and studying the female experience in detail, I find there are women, although not the majority, who find solace and comfort in the lifestyle. Many are drawn to polygamy because it improves the socioeconomic status for themselves and their children. It provides them opportunity to form strong, lasting bonds with other women. For the independent woman, in many cases, it provides respite from the continual, day-in-and-day-out constant dependence on a husband. For the woman who is a teamplayer, it provides solidarity and group cohesion with other co-wives. In short, my studies have shown that polygamy is a viable alternative to the difficulties of single motherhood, spinsterhood, poverty, alienation, and emotional deprivation.

Polygamy is much more difficult for men, who must travel from house to house and task to task, than it is for women, who can share their labors with other women, find time to go to school, seek a career, and have a family. Men must fiercely compete for financial resources and, in the process, often alienate their own sons and other men in the system. They must donate all their resources to the group, defer to the patriarchal council in all things, and struggle to meet the needs of their various families.

Mormon-based polygamy is the most common form of polygamy in North America; however, there are a number of Christian-based groups in Utah and the Intermountain region that are gaining in popularity.

–Janet Bennion, Ph.D., Anthropologist and Author of *Women of Principle: Female Networking in Contemporary Mormon Polygyny*. Oxford University Press.

About the Author

Investigator John R. Llewellyn was a deputy sheriff for twenty-three years in the Salt Lake County Sheriff's Office. He is considered an expert on polygamy cults, and spent a number of years in deep investigation of these organizations. He was often placed on loan to do special investigations for the County Attorney, District Attorney, and Attorney General before those agencies developed their own investigative staffs.

Conducting the preliminary investigation of mass murderer Ervil LeBaron, who was convicted of ordering the murder of Dr. Rulon C. Allred in 1977, Deputy Llewellyn complied an extensive intelligence profile of this infamous polygamist. He also assisted French, British, and local television companies—all wanting to film documentaries—make contact with appropriate members of polygamist groups. Mr. Llewellyn writes feature articles on the subject for newspapers and magazines.

The author pioneered the Morals Squad of the Sheriff Department, which handled the investigation of polygamous complaints. He also wrote a sex crimes manual for the Utah State Police Academy, where he taught Sex Crime Investigation, Interview, and Interrogation.

Mr. Llewellyn is currently the lead investigator in two highly publicized lawsuits against Utah polygamist groups, Apostolic United Brethren, headquartered in Bluffdale, Utah; and The True and Living Church in Manti, Utah.

Investigator Llewellyn is writing his second fact-based novel about the million-dollar corruption within the leadership of some polygamy cults.

He reports that an entrepreneur group is organizing tours to Polygamy groups for the general public and tourists. Their web site will be: www.UtahHistoryTours.com

Coming Soon

The fact-based sequel to Murder of a Prophet is expected to be published in the fall of 2000.

Connie McRae, the estranged wife of Cleveland's Godfather of Gambling is duped of 3.5 million dollars in cash by two members of an infamous polygamous sect. Richard Partridge, the cult leader, wants to create a bogus island nation for gun-running activities with foreign countries. Randal, the other cult member, argues to invest in a brothel on the Utah-Nevada border. Connie's husband, from his prison cell, sends Mafia hit men to recover his money. Detectives Carmichael and Levine become involved in the drama when a polygamist is caught laundering thousands of dollars in cash.